VEILED VENGEANCE

IVY KING

HEARTLEAF PUBLISHING LLC

Veiled Vengeance
The Devils of New York, Book 3
Published by Heartleaf Publishing LLC
Copyright © 2025 by Ivy King
All rights reserved.

Copy/Line Editing by Caitlin Lengerich
Cover Design by Echo Grace - Wildheart Graphics

 Formatted with Vellum

To the real life Abuela,
I miss you something fierce. Thanks for always encouraging me to create. I
love you.
RIP.

TROPES & CONTENT WARNINGS

Tropes
Why choose, MMFM, age gap, touch her and die, touch me and die, morally gray characters, feminine rage

Content Warnings
Torture
Sexual Assault & Attempted Sexual Assault
Gang Rape
Blackmail
Human Trafficking
Primal Play
Anxiety
Matricide
Kidnapping
Elements of PTSD

SPANISH TRANSLATIONS

Bien hecho – Well done

Cabrón – bastard

Cállete – shut up

Eres mi reina – You are my queen

Esa es una hermosa vista. La podría ver todos los días. – Now that's a beautiful site. I could look at it all day.

Eso dolió – That hurt

Esperemos que tenga información para nosotros. – Here's to hoping he has information for us.

Estoy bien – I'm okay

Hijo de puta – son of a bitch

Hombre – man

La mara – the gang

Mierda – shit

Nada – nothing

Ni en un million años – Not in a million years

Ni te atrevas – Don't you dare

¿Ni un hola a tu hermano mayor? – No hello for your big brother?

No soy estúpido. – I'm not stupid.
No te preocupes – Don't worry about it.
Nunca me vuelvas a hacer – Don't ever do that to me again.
Pendejo – asshole
Quítarte la blusa ahora – Take off your shirt now
Serás mi muerte – You'll be the death of me
Sí, por favor – Yes, please
Sobre mi cadaver – Over my dead body
Te amo – I love you
Tú nos perteneces – You belong to us.
Vamos, viejo. – Come on, old man.

PLAYLIST

I Ran (So Far Away) by Hidden Citizens
Inferno by Bella Porch & Sub Urban
White Flag by Bishop Briggs
I'm Gonna Be by Post Malone
Roses (feat. ROZES) by The Chainsmokers
MACHINE by Neoni
Slayer by Bryce Savage
Living Hell by Bella Porch
Rambo by Bryson Tiller
Him & I by G-Eazy & Halsey
I Like Me Better by Lauv
I See You by MISSIO
Gotta Love It by Ruelle
Bad Side by Hidden Citizens, Kazu & Ranya
Dark Side by Bishop Briggs

PROLOGUE

ANTHONY, THREE YEARS AGO

The smell of cheap cigars and grocery store perfume permeates the air of the car, setting my teeth on edge. The driver isn't much better. He's in his late fifties, and someone should have taken his driver's license a long time ago. The ride has been so bumpy that I almost spilled my coffee all over my Armani suit.

When I arrived at Teterboro this morning, I didn't expect it would take hours to get into the city. It's fucking absurd.

My personal assistant booked this car service for me—guess it's time to fire her. I know an oil tycoon who would pay top dollar to break her.

The horrendous noise of New York City is adding to the headache I've had for the last week. Ever since I came home from a business meeting to find Spencer's half of the closet empty, I've been scouring the country for her. Finding her stuff gone was like a stab to my stomach—I couldn't breathe.

I've called in every favor and even gave out IOUs. I don't like owing people, but I'm desperate. If owing that piece of shit at The Company means I'll finally have my Flower in my arms again, I'll do it. I just might have to take something else from The Company to ensure the IOU isn't cashed in for a favor I don't want to do.

The driver puts the car in park and turns his head to me. "We're here, Mr. Cole. I'll come open your door."

At least he knows how to do *that*. If only he knew how to keep his fucking limo from smelling like two-dollar hookers and wannabe thugs.

As I step out, through the open door, he asks, "Should I just wait here?"

Refusing to satisfy his question with a response, I narrow my eyes and walk past him to the employee waiting for me in the dingy coffee shop. The sign above the store reads, "The Mudhouse."

A fucking ridiculous name for an establishment.

The man I'm looking for sits at a small round table by the window.

Chad has been in my employ for less than a year. Normally, I wouldn't make the trip for a meeting with someone so low on my totem pole, but he claims to have the information I need.

When he sees me, he jumps to his feet, almost knocking over the nauseating coffee. "Sir, th-thank you for coming," he stammers and pulls out a chair for me.

Taking the seat, I get right to business. "You said you saw her."

Sitting back down, he sips his coffee. "Yes, sir. Just a few streets over, in a flower shop. She said she's the owner."

"What's the name of the shop?"

"Uh, Central Park Blooms."

I narrow my eyes. "And you're sure it was her?"

He nods. "Positive. I even pulled out the picture that was sent around when I saw her."

"Then let's go." Not wanting to wait another minute for the

reunion, I stand and walk out, knowing Chad will be right on my heels. "How far is it?"

He points in the direction I came from. "Just a couple blocks that way."

"We'll take my car."

"Yes, sir."

My fingers tingle as I anticipate the feel of her skin, the smell of her hair. It's been too long since I last had her under me. Blood rushes to my cock as I think about sinking into her again. I'll chain her to our bed and never let her go.

Chad directs the driver to the flower shop. It's so small that if you blink, you'll miss it entirely. There's one large window next to the glass door, but I'm unable to see inside with all the damn flowers on display in the window.

Without a word or direction, Chad follows me into the shop. A bell chimes as we step over the threshold and I lock the door behind us, flipping the sign to read, "Sorry, we're closed."

Lilies, roses, baby's breath, sunflowers, and carnations decorate the room with the colors of the rainbow.

But not a single hyacinth is to be found. The flower for *my* Flower. The symbol that shows her how much I love her—that I'll always come back to her.

My face flushes a shade of red at the thought of her throwing out the symbol of my love for her.

Looks like my Flower didn't learn her lesson.

"I'll be with you in a minute!" a voice calls from an open door that I assume leads to a storeroom.

Chad bounces nervously on the balls of his feet. I glance at him and find a drop of sweat trickling down his temple.

"How can I help you?" A woman steps up to the glass display case that serves as a checkout counter. There's dirt under her nails and smudges on her shirt. Her hair is long, wavy, and a shade of light brown. Her eyes are dark, like chocolate.

I tilt my head to the side. "Are you the owner?"

She holds her hand out for me to shake. "Yes. My name is Natalie Cabrera."

Taking her hand in mine, I question, "Do you have an employee named Spencer?"

Natalie drops my hand. "I don't have any employees. I just opened and haven't had the time to hire anyone."

Spasms of irritation flicker across my face. My words drip with fury. "You said it was her."

Chad's hands shake, and his eyes round with fear. "I—I thought . . ."

"Clearly, you thought wrong!" My voice gets louder with each word.

Natalie jumps back from the counter. "You both need to leave now, please."

"I'm—I'm sorry, sir. I really thought it was her."

Grabbing his cheeks and squeezing them together, I turn his face to Natalie. "You think she looks like my Flower? Her?!"

He tries to speak, but I won't let him, so he shakes his head back and forth vigorously.

Damn right, this woman isn't my Flower. But he should have realized that before he called me.

Bringing my mouth to his ear, I whisper, "You should have looked closer." Before he can react, I slam his head on the display case, shattering the glass. Chad groans, but his eyes don't open.

Natalie screams and attempts to flee. She darts around the display case, heading for the door. I tangle my hand in her long, wavy hair and pull. "Where do you think you're going?"

She cries out in pain. "No! Let me go! Please!" She claws at my hand, trying to get free.

I release her hair and spin her around. The slap I land on her cheek knocks her to the floor. "You're not her!"

Tears pour down her cheeks. "I'm sorry. Please just let me go. I won't tell anyone. Just let me go. I promise I won't say anything."

"I promise. I won't say anything."

Honey eyes are suddenly staring back at me.

"Stop lying! You said that, but then you left! You left me! You didn't even leave a note!" Spittle flies out of my mouth.

"Wha—What? But I—"

I grab the collar of her shirt and pull her to her feet. "Why! I've given you everything! We have one little fight, so you leave?"

Spencer pulls at my hands, trying to peel back my fingers from her shirt. "Please stop. I—I don't know you. I don't know who you are. I'm not who you think I am."

How dare she . . .

My breathing grows ragged. "You don't know me? I'm your fucking fiancé!" I shove her to the ground and grab the first item within reach.

She sobs, and I kneel down next to her. Leaning in close, I plant a soft kiss on her cheek. "I'll never let you forget me." Then I raise both arms and plunge the pruning shears into her stomach.

Her mouth opens with a silent scream. Pain is written across her face.

Good. My Flower needs to feel my pain.

She blinks a few times, and her eyes are no longer honey, they're chocolate.

An enraged scream blows past my lips, and I bring the pruning shears down into the body of the woman below me over and over. Almost every surface in the shop drips red, and

Natalie's eyes remain open and lifeless as she lies there, on the ground.

A groan draws my attention to the man rolling over the broken glass. Chad attempts to crawl towards the door, so I stand and grab his foot, pulling him next to Natalie. "You lied!"

He holds his hands out in front of him, hoping to ward me off. "I'm sorry, sir. I'm really sorry. Please. I'll—I'll make it up to you."

"Too late." I grab his hair at the crown of his head and pull back, exposing his neck. Then I drag the point of the shears across his exposed skin. Arterial blood sprays my face.

A tattered breath passes through my lungs as I pocket the shears and pull my handkerchief out of my suit pocket.

What the stupid shows on TV don't tell you is that blood doesn't wash off easily, and now my suit is ruined. I wipe the handkerchief across my face and leave the shop.

My driver is leaning against the car but jumps when he sees me. His lips part in surprise. "Are you okay, Mr. Cole? Should I take you to the hospital?"

I shake my head. "Back to Teterboro."

"Are you sure? You're covered in—"

My jaw tenses. "You're not paid to ask questions. You're paid to drive. Now drive."

"Yes, Mr. Cole."

I sigh, sinking into the leather seat.

It's too bad he's seen too much.

CHAPTER 1

SPENCER

I can't feel anything.

I think this is what psychologists call disassociation. I'm unable to scrounge up an ounce of care—not even for Iris, my friend. I should be strong for her; she's been one of my main supports this year. I should tell her that I will get us out of this. I *have* to get us out of this.

"Iris?" I hiss at her. She still isn't awake, but moans.

"Ignore her, Flower."

"Iris, wake up," I try again.

The sun is now firmly over the horizon. The light illuminates the discoloration on Asher's and Iris's skin. The dry blood on Asher's temple, nose, and lip has turned a dark rust hue. The heat from the summer air hugs the windows from the outside, but the chill of the room clings to my skin, covering my body in goosebumps.

Asher looks to me with his one swollen eye. Pity fills his face as he cautions me. "Spencer, no." He shakes his head, warning me to stop.

Stop what? Stop trying? I can't. My mom . . . No. Not yet. I'll think about that later.

Anthony turns his back to me while he takes a phone call and gives more orders to his men.

"I'm going to get us out of here. Don't worry," I assure him in hushed tones.

"Rio and Zane will come for us—we discussed this. We just need to survive until they get here."

"There's only two of them, and Anthony has more than ten men here. Those aren't good odds. And Iris . . ." Doubt settles into my chest.

Anthony claps his hands. "Well, let's get down to it, shall we?"

My body goes rigid remembering the "training" he discussed and attempted last night. "No," I whisper in fear. But I notice his attention is not on me, but on Iris.

Anthony snaps his fingers. "Get her up."

Two men haul her up by her arms and raise her bound wrists over her head. They grab a hook hanging from the ceiling and attach the tape to her wrists. Her toes barely scrape the ground and she moans again at the pain.

Anthony viciously grabs her face, pinching her cheeks together. "Sweet, sweet Dahlia. Such a disappointment." When he lets go, he throws her face to the side.

My lips purse together tightly.

Dahlia?

Anthony picks up on my uncertainty and a smug look crosses his face as he turns to me. "Didn't you know? Dahlia here is one of my most trusted employees."

My heart hollows out. I'm empty. "Iris?"

"I'm so sorry . . ." she chokes out, her eyes barely open. "I didn't want to."

Tears of betrayal sting my eyes. My trusted friend. I let her in.

Is this all my life is meant to be? Everyone lies. Everyone keeps secrets. Am I that dumb and ignorant? Am I that desperate that I'm such an easy target?

Anthony's sugary tone leaves a sour taste in my mouth. "Oh, we both know that's not true. You'd do anything, *have* done anything, just to see him."

I don't want to give into the bait, but I can't help myself. I deserve answers. "Him?"

Anthony's face brightens as I give in to his narrative. "Her son."

Son?! But Iris . . . *Dahlia* is only nineteen!

"It's a good thing she kept her figure after she had him, or else I would've had to terminate her employment early." He twirls a lock of her hair between his fingers. "It's too bad she failed, though. She wasn't supposed to let you get close to those . . . heathens." He spits out the last word like it's diseased and glares at Asher.

"You didn't . . . specify that . . . when you told me . . . to watch her . . . ." Iris is barely able to get out her words. She wheezes and coughs as blood trickles from the corner of her mouth.

That's not good . . .

The slap is loud and echoes off the cement walls and glass windows, jolting me in my chair. Asher clenches his jaw, and his fists go taut. Dahlia's head whips to the side from the force of Anthony's hand.

"Don't get technical with me—you're on a short leash. Your little act of rebellion is going to cost you." Anthony goes from self-satisfied to incensed in less than a second. His moods are unpredictable and make me feel on edge.

"I did just as . . . you asked. Let me see my August . . . I want to see him . . ." Dahlia croaks out.

I feel more than see the punch to her torso. I wince at the impact while Dahlia coughs up more blood. The concern for her wellbeing shouldn't be there—I should be angry with her. But right next to the betrayal in my heart sits sympathy, and it's growing larger with each word from her mouth.

She has a *son*, and it sounds like Anthony keeps him away from her. I may not be a mother, but I know what I would do for those I love. And knowing that Anthony runs a human trafficking ring? I can't imagine what is happening to that little boy.

But what do I know? Up until a minute ago, I didn't even know Iris's—*Dahlia's* real name. What was fake, and what was real with us?

Anthony grips Dahlia's hair at the crown of her head and yanks her head back as far as it'll go. She lets out a scratchy, gurgled yelp. The angle is uncomfortable just to watch; I can't imagine the pain she's in. "If you think I'm going to let you see him after you failed to deliver on your end, you're horribly mistaken." He drops her hair like it burned him.

"Fuck . . . You . . ."

Anthony shakes his head side to side. "Tsk, tsk. Dahlia, Dahlia, Dahlia. You know better than to talk to me like that. Sounds like you need to learn another lesson." He snaps his fingers again, and the same two men from before walk forward to where Dahlia hangs.

Dahlia collects what little energy she has. She opens her eyes again and shoots a withering look toward Anthony. "Bring it."

Anthony releases a derisive laugh and addresses the two men but maintains eye contact with Dahlia. "Have at her, gentlemen."

"Don't look, Spencer," Asher demands, but I ignore him. I won't leave Dahlia alone in this moment. I was alone before—no one deserves that emptiness. The people who take are already leaving her with nothing; I don't have to do the same. It doesn't matter what she's done to me, I won't turn my back on her. No one deserves to be alone when they already feel helpless and weak.

Dahlia's eyes meet mine. The fear there is unmistakable, but it quickly fades, and resolve replaces it.

One of the men unbuckles his belt while the other yanks down Dahlia's pants without care. For the next hour or more, the room is a rotating door of various *employees* taking turns with Dahlia's body. She doesn't let out a single cry. Tears leak from the corners of her eyes, but she remains stoic. Each teardrop of her eye pairs with ten or more of my own. Asher trembles with irate energy as each man finishes with Dahlia.

Anthony watches the entire scene like it's a nighttime sitcom, telling each man "good job" when they're done.

This isn't the first time she's endured this—that much is evident. But I'll make sure it's her last.

CHAPTER 2

ASHER

*A*nthony Fucking Cole is going to die. Slowly. Painfully. I'll make sure of it.

I hated him before—more than any other person I have ever known. But now, the hate in my soul has found a new level.

Dahlia.

I should have seen it. I should have known.

Spencer isn't a trained CIA operative. No matter how hard she tries to keep the attention off herself, there's no way for her to go unnoticed in a crowded room. Anthony was bound to find her, and the fact that she remained hidden from him for almost three years is either a testament to her vigilance or his stupidity.

With how busy Anthony is, of course he planted someone in Spencer's life to watch her. But from what I could tell, there was no malice to be found in Dahlia's friendship with Spencer. Even now . . . She knew what would happen when she didn't follow Anthony's unspoken orders.

She passed out from the pain just moments after the last man left.

Anthony watches her unconscious body with a triumphant glee. When he turns to me, his face changes instantly. Revulsion takes over his features.

"Your turn."

I shrug. "Sorry. I don't think I'm their type."

Anthony's eyes narrow to slits. "If that's how you want to play it." He snaps his fingers, and two more of his men approach me. They use a couple of pocket knives to cut the tape binding me to the chair, then secure my wrists together with more tape. I let them because I know what's coming next. I need my strength.

"What are you doing to him? Leave him alone! Don't touch him!" Spencer thrashes in her chair next to me. The tape digs into her skin—her precious skin.

"Shut up!" Anthony backhands her.

She better not have scars after this—she doesn't need the reminder. And if she does, I'll have to figure out how to bring Anthony back from the dead so I can kill him all over again.

My wrists are lifted above my head and attached to a hook, just like the one Dahlia is hanging from. One man tugs on a chain a few feet away, and I'm lifted up from the chair. The man has to give the chain another tug to make it so I'm dangling with the tips of my shoes hovering just above the cold floor.

The pressure around my wrists is uncomfortable but bearable. It's the searing pain that radiates from my shoulder that makes me almost black out. The bleeding has stopped, but the movement causes a fresh gush of blood to pour from my wound. The recovery from this shit isn't going to be fun, but I'll manage.

I imagine pulling the pain from my body and shoving it into

a box. I lock the lid, throw away the key, and the box gets stored in the back of my mind.

It'd be nice if Rio and Zane would hurry the fuck up.

"Stop it!"

Tilting my head back, I turn to her. "It's all right, Princess. I'm fine." My voice is more strained than I intend.

Anthony pulls out a set of brass knuckles and places them on his right hand. I see the blow to my ribs coming a mile away. I harden my abs to lessen the damage, but the impact still stings. I can't stop the grunt that makes its way past my lips. "Like butterfly kisses," I mutter.

"Don't make me tell you again. Don't talk to her! She's not your *Princess;* she's not your *anything*!"

I chuckle, knowing my lack of cowering is only going to enrage him further. But the more his attention is on me, the less it'll be on her.

"Getting started without me?" Pierce strolls in through the metal door and stops when he's shoulder to shoulder with Anthony. The hurt on his face is genuine, as if he actually feels left out.

Fucking psychopaths.

"We need answers," Anthony says without remorse.

"Then allow me to help." Pierce pulls out his own set of brass knuckles.

Anthony gestures to my vulnerable frame. "Be my guest."

"Leave him alone! Please!" Spencer's terror is palpable and fills the room. I need her to remain calm, but I can't give her the cue now. Drawing attention to herself is only going to cause her pain.

Anthony sneers at Spencer. "You need to learn what happens when you fool around with trash, Flower."

Pierce's jabs and punches to my torso make me feel like I've gone twelve rounds with Muhammed Ali, but I try to keep the groans and hisses to a minimum because each one causes Spencer to flinch. Somewhere along the way, I think he fractures a rib.

"That's enough, Pierce." Anthony's tone has an air of finality, but Pierce keeps punishing my torso with his blows. "I said, that's enough!" Anthony grips Pierce by the shoulder and yanks. Pierce turns with his fist raised.

"I wasn't done," Pierce says through panting breaths.

Anthony's glower says he isn't too happy at being defied in front of others. "We need him to talk. He can't do that if you beat the shit out of him." He snaps his fingers again.

I'm getting really tired of his air of entitlement with those finger snaps.

A man with a rolling metal table comes forward from the shadows. On the table is an array of knives. I think the move is supposed to scare me, but I've been friends with Rio for over ten years. Rio's *creativity* with a blade is intimidating. A couple of rich boys who grew up with a silver spoon won't make me sweat.

My head hangs forward as I chuckle.

Pierce jerks my head up by my hair. "You won't be laughing much longer." My neck strains, but I keep laughing.

Anthony throws another punch at my midsection, effectively putting a stop to my laughter. "Now that that's over, tell me something: What does the FBI know about our operations?"

My breathing is labored. They may not scare me, but, shit, I'm fucking sore. "Which operations would that be?"

"We both know the FBI sent Dustin to Euphoria wearing a wire. Tell me what else you know."

Wow. He really is a dumbass.

If the FBI had the recording, he would have been taken into custody already. Considering the shit he revealed about stalking Spencer and admitting to blackmailing two NYPD officers, he would've been collared right away.

"A wire?"

The more I get him to admit to me, the deeper the hole he digs for himself. I can't use the recording from Euphoria, because proving that Dustin consented to the recording will be difficult since he's dead. With New York being a single-party consent state, if Rio would've gotten his head out of his ass and had Dustin sign a damn piece of paper, I could have taken that recording right to the FBI. But now, even if I could trust everyone in my office, the recording would be inadmissible.

"The wire Dustin wore into Euphoria!"

"He's not going to talk," Pierce mutters.

Anthony picks up one of the knives, but his grip on the handle is all wrong. I let my head fall forward, and I smirk.

Just like I thought. A couple of rich men playing at torture experts.

Anthony slashes at my arm with the knife, leaving behind a shallow cut. My sweat trickles into the open graze. The burn is inconvenient, but I barely notice it.

"Tell me! What does the FBI know about our trafficking operation?" He's losing his patience, which is just what I need. I will happily play the part of the FBI idiot to get him talking.

"Weapons trafficking?" Another cut stings on my arm.

"Human! Human trafficking! Your two little roommates have been fucking things up for us for years! They've raided my parties in Bushwick and Hoboken."

Pierce rests a hand on the metal table and leans. "It's a good thing they haven't found the prep houses on Long Island."

"Shut up, Pierce!" Anthony turns back to me. His eyes are deranged; he's quickly losing control. "Tell me what the FBI knows." He rests the blade on my arm and applies pressure, but he doesn't break the skin. It's a threat—a horrible threat, but a threat, nonetheless.

"What kind of details are you looking for?" I put a little quiver in my voice. Spencer whimpers and calls out for me again, but I ignore her. Anthony is so focused on me that he doesn't hear her either.

"Do they know about the prep houses on Long Island? Do they know about the officials we have under our thumb? Do they know about the list? Has Spencer given them the list?"

Here goes a shot in the dark.

"Your client list?"

"Yes!" His face blazes with barely restrained rage.

Definitely an idiot and losing control. He's given me more information in the last few minutes than we've learned in the last few years.

I change the subject. "The news is calling you 'The Bride Butcher.'"

"Stupid name. I should professionally crucify whoever came up with it," he sneers.

Pushing the subject further, I give him more of what we know. "You've murdered five women from the east to the west coast. Selling women isn't enough for you? You have to murder them too?"

His eyes glaze over as he gets caught up in his memories. "Actually, it's seven, and I was just trying to find Spencer! Every state I visited, every city, I looked for her. It took me over two years to find her. There were times I thought I spotted her, but it always turned out to be another."

"You killed women because you couldn't find me? That's your excuse?" Spencer chimes in.

"You shouldn't have run!" Spittle flies from his mouth as his attention and wrath turn to her.

Not good.

"I gave you everything. Everything! You wanted for nothing! And you decided to test me by forcing me to play this ridiculous cat-and-mouse game!" His ire is thrown at Spencer like a spear. He means to cut her to the quick, but his delusion doesn't account for the fact that she doesn't love him.

"So, you killed them and put them in my wedding dress? You apparently love me so much that you killed and raped them?"

"Spencer," I warn. She's entering dangerous territory. If his fantasy shatters, Anthony will lose all sense of control and lash out at the object of his affection.

Her.

Spencer's eyes are wide with shock as she ignores me. "You're insane," she whispers.

Anthony raises his hand to strike, but I yell out before he can strike.

"Do you really think I'd tell you anything? Anthony Cole. Orphan. University of Texas graduate. Rich from Mommy and Daddy's money. You think that just because you have money and privilege, you can fucking *sell* people."

Anthony's eyes darken, and a knowing smirk grazes his lips. He shows no remorse for any of his actions. "And what about you, FBI Agent Asher Wolfgang Dawson? Your mother was nothing more than a two-dollar whore, pimped out by your father."

I grind my teeth together to prevent myself from giving him the reaction he wants.

"And then there's your college sweetheart. Rachel? You shared her with your dirty friends, too, just like you tried sharing my Flower. Is that why she killed herself? She couldn't stand the thought of spreading her legs for someone who was practically born in the gutter and couldn't provide the lifestyle she was accustomed to living?"

My gut clenches as I recall finding her lifeless body with one of my belts wrapped around her neck.

Condescension oozes from his voice. "Or was it because of the assault from the football captain? Poor little Asher couldn't save Rachel from her own mind after that. And Rachel couldn't handle the stain on her reputation it brought, could she?"

My breath billows from my teeth, and my knuckles turn white.

"You don't know what you're talking about."

"But I do, don't I?"

My eyes subtly slide to Spencer. I don't want to know what she thinks of my upbringing; I wouldn't be able to handle the rejection from my partner again. But I can't help myself.

When our gazes meet, she looks at me with the same look from the other night. Sympathy.

Anthony moves closer towards my dangling body. He brandishes the knife again so he can intimidate the answers out of me.

That's not going to work.

When he's close enough, I tighten my abs and grip the hook. A set of feet come into my line of sight. Ignoring the agonizing burn in my shoulder, I kick out with my right leg. My foot connects with Anthony's torso. A grunt is forced from his lips, and he doubles over.

Pierce lunges forward and aims his armored fist at my bullet wound. The sound that bursts from my mouth is full of agony. I've been ignoring the fire burning in my shoulder until now. The box of pain has been forcefully opened, and I'm struggling to close the lid again. More blood streams down from my open wound.

"No! Stop! Please! I'll do anything! Just stop hurting him!"

No one gives Spencer's pleas recognition. Anthony and Pierce are too focused on me.

Just how I want them to be.

Anthony stands. His hair is disheveled and there's a distinct, muddy boot print on his shirt. He lands a few blows of his own straight to my stomach in retaliation. It's becoming more difficult to keep my torso tight so as to not allow serious damage.

When Anthony finally stops, he straightens and smooths his hair. My shirt is soaked in sweat and blood.

"Come, Pierce. Let's give Agent Dawson some time to think over his answers." He slips the brass knuckles into his pocket and saunters out of the warehouse. Pierce's wandering eyes linger on Spencer, dipping to the cleavage her dress reveals.

He's going to regret his ogling. Even if Spencer doesn't want me after we get out here, and after learning about my history, I'll still protect her from the Anthony's and Pierce's of the world. Men like that think they can take just because they want.

"Asher," Spencer whispers. "Asher, please, stay awake."

But my eyes droop closed. The box is spilling over with pain now—it's becoming impossible to keep the lid locked in place.

"I'll be back for you, my Lily." Pierce's promise is spoken low so only Spencer and me are able to hear him. Forcing my eyes to remain open, I watch Spencer's frame shake as she swallows a gulp of fear. Pierce smiles at her reaction and finally stalks out after Anthony.

With the immediate threat gone, pain finally claims my consciousness.

CHAPTER 3

ZANE

My heart feels like it's been ripped out of my chest, beat with a bat, then handed back to me, as if I can still make it function. My Angel is gone, along with my best friend.

When the gunshots rang out, my entire world came to a halt. Rio and I rushed to get to Asher and Spencer, but we were too late. They got them in the car and drove away.

Someone at the gallery called 9-1-1, so we had to give statements. Liam came running when he heard what had happened over the radio, and so did Asher's teammates, Berkowitz and Kowalski. We all went into search-and-rescue mode.

Rio and I haven't slept all night.

We filled them in on Anthony. We didn't relay the human trafficking aspect, but they know he's rich, connected, and psychotic. And with the positive match from the DNA test, everyone knows that Spencer's attacker and the Bride Butcher are the same person. We still need a sample of Anthony's DNA to prove that Anthony is the Bride Butcher, but for now, we're all operating under that assumption.

Now, it's late—or maybe it's early morning. I've lost all sense of time. Spencer and Asher have been gone for hours, but it feels like years.

Rio and I are sitting in my car at the edge of Central Park. The moon is high, and there's a small chill in the air. We haven't changed out of the clothes we wore to the show and probably look as deranged and haggard as we feel.

Rio breaks the silence. "He wasn't too happy to talk to us last time."

"And he probably won't be happy to talk to us this time," I retort.

"*Esperemos que tenga información para nosotros,*" he mumbles and exits the car. *Here's hoping he has information for us.*

"Here's hoping," I add, then follow suit.

For once, Hank isn't with a customer. A cigarette hangs from his mouth, the end glowing red in the night. He jerks back like he's been slapped when he sees us coming, but he quickly schools his features.

"Back so soon?"

I don't have time for niceties or manners. I'm not sure I had much of those to begin with, but whatever crumbs of them I had are gone.

I grab Hank by the front of his shirt, my fists gathering the fabric and gripping hard, and I slam his body against the tree. Rio leers at Hank over my shoulder.

"What the fuck, man?!" Panic makes its way into his voice. Hank finally looks at me, really looks at me, and sees the dark circles under my eyes. He sees my untamed hair, my desperation.

"We're not going to do our usual song and dance, Hanky Boy. This is a simple question-and-answer visit."

"Are you on something?"

I grit my teeth; I don't have time for bullshit. Spencer and

Asher don't have time either. "No. Now, answer my questions. What have you heard about Cain?"

"Him again? Come on, Zane, I told you everything I know last time."

I slam him again. "You know something! You have to know something!"

Hank holds up his hands. "I don't—"

Rio steps forward and pulls out one of his knives. He holds the blade to Hank's throat. "You're no chump, Hank. You *know* something. Tell us. No detail is too small or inconsequential."

"Okay, okay! God!" He sighs a deep frustrated breath. "White Plains."

"What?" I tilt my head to the side.

"White Plains," he repeats.

"I don't have time for your half-assed shit! What are you talking about!"

"They might be in White Plains! There's someone up there buying a ton of warehouses. I think Cain is scrambling to move his stables because of you."

Rio scrunches his eyebrows. "Us?"

"I think you're getting closer to finding him and shutting down his ring."

I release his shirt, and we turn and walk away without handing over payment or offering a thanks.

Like I said, I didn't have any manners to begin with.

RIO HOPPED in the driver's seat when we got to the car. A move that—any other day—would have started a brawl right there in the street, but I'm a mess. Rio is too, but he seems more equipped to drive than I do.

We haven't even attempted to turn on the radio and argue over song choice—we drive in silence.

I startle when I realize where we are.

I give Rio a puzzled look. "You're going the wrong way."

"No, I'm not."

"White Plains is not located on our street."

Rio nods. "I know that. I passed geography in school." He pulls up in front of our brownstone.

"Then what the hell are we doing here?"

Rio turns off the engine and pulls the keys out of the ignition. "We're here because you need food, I need food, you need a shower, and I need a shower. Then lastly, we can't go up into White Plains, guns blazing—we're not cowboys. You need to do your computer genius thing and look this shit up. We'll make a plan and then go get them."

He's right. We have to be smart about this. I need to verify the warehouse purchases and narrow down which one they're at.

I sigh and lean my head back against the headrest. "You're right. We'll plan."

Rio's hand dives into my hair and pulls my face to his. His lips find mine easily and offer me the comfort and reassurance I need. I open my mouth and our tongues dance together and I return the same confidence he so freely gives me.

When we pull apart, our foreheads connect, and we breathe together, connecting in a way that calms us both.

"We've got this," Rio whispers.

"We've got this," I echo back.

I'M TOWELING my hair with another around my waist when there's banging on the front door. Rio is already dressed and downstairs, so I rush down the steps in my barely-dressed glory with my gun in hand.

Rio is at the door, weapon in hand, chatting away with whoever is on the other side. I come up behind him and find the last person I expected to see.

Hayes.

Rio leans an arm on the doorframe. "How did you find our address?"

Hayes narrows his eyes. "You're not the only one with connections."

My brows shoot up. What the hell is he talking about? I did Hayes's background check and found nothing of importance. Yet here he is, claiming he can somehow get the same kind of information we have access to.

I finally chime into the conversation. "And you're here . . . why?"

He balls his fists at his sides. "I know you know where she is."

After a long pause, I ask, "Spencer?"

"Iris! She's missing; I can't reach her. I went by her apartment, and it was torn apart—it's completely trashed." His despair matches my own.

"We had nothing to do with whatever has happened to her."

"I know that!" He rests his hands on his hips, his head falling forward, and he takes a deep breath. "I need to find her."

"Come on. Get in here." Rio reaches for his shoulder and guides Hayes inside. Rio tries to guide Hayes to the couch to sit, but he refuses.

"Please just . . ." Hayes pinches the bridge of his nose. "Tell me what you know. I need to know." He crosses his arms and plants his feet, effectively communicating his determination.

"You should let us handle this," I offer. Hayes is young, way too young to get caught up in all of this.

"Like hell," he scoffs.

Gotta give credit where credit's due.

Rio and I share a look. We've been together and worked together long enough that I know what each of his micro-expressions mean. I send a small nod back that gives my agreement.

Rio turns to Hayes first. "Spencer and Asher were taken by the Bride Butcher."

"The Bride Butcher? The serial killer that's been all over the news?"

I internally roll my eyes. I hate the media, especially Sherry, and the shit she tried pulling with Asher.

"That's the one," Rio answers.

Hayes proves not to be a dumbass when he asks the right questions. "Why them?"

I give the easy answer and let him draw his own conclusion. "The Bride Butcher is Spencer's ex, Anthony Cole."

Hayes speaks slowly, as if he's talking to himself aloud. "So, the man who attacked Spencer was her ex, who has been killing women for years . . ." He trails off and turns around, giving us his back. He runs his hands through his hair.

Rio takes a step toward him. "You know it's not her fault, right?"

Hayes spins back around. "Yeah, I know. This is just . . . a lot." He stares at the ground, working out the puzzle. His head snaps up, and he questions, "She ran away from him? That's why she ended up here?"

"It's not really our story to tell," I answer him.

He nods, accepting my response as sufficient. "Okay, okay . . . And you know where they are?"

"We don't know that Anthony has Iris," I explain.

Hayes shakes his head, jarring the doubt from his mind. "No. He has her; I know it. He took Asher. He had to have taken Iris too."

"If she's there, we'll get her back for you," Rio promises.

Hayes startles, walking toward us. "No, I'm going with you."

"No way," I add forcefully, holding my hand out to stop him.

"You leave me behind, and I'll just follow you," he threatens.

Rio raises a brow. "We could just tie you up and throw you in the basement."

"You could try. But you're not the only one with tricks up their sleeve." He lifts his shirt, showing us the gun resting in the waistband of his pants.

I grab his arm and guide him to lower his shirt. "Where the hell did you get that? Do you even know how to use it?"

"I've known how to shoot since I was eight. I know the names of each part of the gun, and I know how to disassemble and reassemble it with my eyes closed."

Rio and I become impossibly still. I tilt my head and narrow my eyes. "Your last name isn't Brown, is it?"

Hayes flattens his lips. "No, it's not Brown."

"I figured when I couldn't find much but the basics in a background check. Who are you?"

"Fuck." He runs another hand through his hair. He paces back and forth, three steps in each direction. "Just promise you won't go crazy; I'm not my family."

My muscles tense, and the glower on my face doesn't let up.

I don't like where this is going . . .

"My name is Declan Hayes O'Connell."

Rio's jaw drops. "O'Connell? As in Patrick O'Connell, leader of the IRA?"

Hayes's eyes wander to the ceiling. "Yeah, that's Dad. He's a gem," he says sarcastically. "So . . . I'm coming with, right?"

Rio and I share another communicative look, and I sigh. "This rescue isn't an official NYPD or FBI operation. You get shot, the bill is yours."

Hayes nods his head. "Okay. No problem."

"And one more thing," I add. "You stay out of the way, and you follow exactly what we say."

Hayes bounces on the balls of his feet. "Got it. When do we leave?"

I gesture to myself. "I need to get dressed, man."

CHAPTER 4

SPENCER

*A*sher's limp body gently sways from side to side. I need him to wake up. I need to tell him that his upbringing and past relationships don't dictate ours. But I know his body needs the rest. Each punch Anthony and Pierce delivered to Asher's abdomen felt like I was taking a hit to my own body.

And it happened because of me.

Anthony is going to continue to attempt to drive a wedge between us, but I won't let him. Asher is a good man, no matter what he or anyone else says. A bad man doesn't guard a woman night and day when she's in danger. A bad man doesn't cook a woman's favorite meals for her.

I take up sentry from my taped prison. I may not be able to stop the blows from coming, but I can still watch out for him.

Iris—*Dahlia* slowly blinks sleep from her eyes and scans the room. There's only one guard by the door, but he's not paying any attention to us. I'm pretty sure he's playing a game on his phone.

She sucks in a painful breath as she tries to loosen her stiff muscles. "How long have I been out?"

"A couple hours, I think." The guard Anthony left with us hasn't been rotated out, and the sun has disappeared from my line of sight. If we're going by last night's timetable, then we're probably about halfway or so through his shift.

Her voice lacks emotion. "I'm sorry you had to see all of that."

That's what she chooses to say right now? She's sorry I watched her get gang raped? She's the one with blood and dried sperm on the inside of her thighs, and she's apologizing to me?

I know she's not being sarcastic—it's probably exhaustion mixed with shock or trauma. I may not know this version of her, but I'm not stupid. She's been through shit and probably seen more than her fair share of the ugliness this world has to offer.

But she's apologizing to me for her getting raped?

"I'm sorry that happened to you." Those are the only words I seem to be able to get past my bewilderment.

"You're probably angry with me." Her eyes drop to the floor.

Am I? Yes.

Am I going to tell her that? No.

From what Anthony said, it sounds like she had no choice but to spy on me. But did she have to pretend to be my friend?

She reads my expression like the front page of the New York Times. "It wasn't all fake. I was as real with you as I could be. But . . ."

"Your son." I say it like I still can't believe it, because I can't.

She gives me a half smile. "Yeah. If I did well, then Anthony was going to let me see him."

I want to be angry with her, but how can I kick someone

when they're already down? And she's not just down. She was shoved in the sewer and forced to lie in the filth.

I try to keep things casual, but I can't stop certain questions from slipping out. "Your real name is Dahlia?"

"Yeah. Dahlia Monroe."

I nod my head as if that makes perfect sense when really, I'm freaking out right now. The betrayal hurts, but it's more like a dull ache. A discomfort that will be gone in less than a week.

"And you have a son? But you're only nineteen."

She takes a heaving breath, and her eyes gather tears. "August is three years old. I had him when I was sixteen."

"Were you . . ." How do I ask someone about the details of their tragic past? Someone I know, but don't know.

"Kidnapped? Yes. I was taken when I was walking home from school."

"Are you from New York? Wouldn't someone have recognized you here?"

"No. I'm from Los Angeles. I got pregnant with August soon after that."

This isn't making sense. "But how—"

She answers me before I can get the question out. "Anthony had a client—I guess you can call him that—that Anthony said called me his favorite. He didn't use a condom like he was supposed to. Anthony almost killed me for getting pregnant— like it was my fault. But he didn't because he discovered some men have a fetish for pregnant women. I was just a teenager, but Anthony has always gotten plenty of business because of me."

My stomach rolls, and bile threatens to come up from my stomach. She was forced into this life and had no way out. "You're still only nineteen."

Dahlia's half-smirk brightens her face. "At times, I feel much older than that."

Duh, Spencer. Way to put your foot in your mouth.

"I'm sorry you got hurt because—"

She shakes her head. "It's not your fault. I knew what I was doing when he sent me to you back in January. I knew what I was risking by not following all of his rules."

Shit. She's a better person than most. "Is your son going to be okay?"

A special strength flashes in her eyes. "Yeah. Anthony won't hurt August. He knows he can't control me if he does."

I *really* don't want to go down that line of questioning.

We lapse into silence because there's nothing else to say. I'll probably have a million more questions once we get out of here, but for now, she's given me what I need to continue trusting her.

Calling her by her real name will be weird and take some time to get used to.

How many different aliases has Anthony made her take on? How many Spencers has Dahlia had to spy on?

I know the answers won't bring me comfort, and they won't help us get out of here.

Rio and Zane need to hurry the fuck up.

CHAPTER 5

SPENCER

I drift off to sleep when the adrenaline finally leaves my body, and a small headache squeezes my head, forcing my eyes closed. The sun finally set, and I should be on guard, but I haven't eaten, and I haven't slept yet since we were taken. My body can only go without so much.

Sleep doesn't cradle me for long before a bang from the metal doors jerks us all awake. The sun is shining directly in my eyes, keeping my vision blurred. I peek at Asher, his face is grim as he looks at whoever has entered. A thump reaches my ears as the sound of footsteps on pavement get closer to my chair. Despite the warmth, a chill snakes up my spine, and goosebumps break out across my arms.

A form blocks the sun, and I blink rapidly, allowing my eyes to adjust. Pierce Murphy's gleeful face swims into view.

"My Lily, I'm here." He squats down, grabs my face, and kisses me. His touch is hard and punishing. "We don't have long to do this." He looks deep into my eyes. Adoration glistens in his eyes.

The urge to retch claws at my throat. "What are you talking

about?" I search the room for an escape even though I'm still taped to the chair. I spot the man who was standing guard at the door. He's lying unconscious on the ground.

Fuck.

With his hands still on my face, his thumbs swipe across my cheekbones. "We can finally be together."

Is he serious?

My mouth opens and closes repeatedly. "Pierce, I—"

"I see the way you look at me—the way you've *always* looked at me. You want this just as much as I do." His eyes wander down to the front of my dress and dip into my cleavage. "Anthony is busy in the city; this is the only time we have."

"What?"

"Don't you fucking touch her!" Asher thrashes about, and the chain around his hook clanks loudly.

His hands go to the front of my dress and grip the neckline at the center of my chest. With a yank, my breasts spill out. My heart flips, and a stab of terror slices through my sternum.

This can't be happening. Please. Not again. I can't survive this again.

"Please don't do this," I whimper. Black tears roll down my cheeks as saltwater mixes with my mascara.

"Shhh." He holds a finger up to my mouth. "It's okay. I know you don't love him like you love me."

"No. Please no," I beg.

"I know you love me."

Oh my God. He's delusional.

Fuck this. I'm not going down without a fight.

"No, I don't!" I shout. Spit flies from my mouth and lands on his face.

Pierce blinks, and his fist goes right into my stomach. "Stop lying! You're lying"

I wheeze. "I don't want you. I never wanted you."

"Yes, you do! Admit it!" Pierce continues to punch my abdomen.

Asher doesn't let up as he fights to break free. "Stop! Get your filthy hands off her, you piece of shit! You pathetic piece of shit!"

I can barely breathe as Pierce wrenches my thighs apart and pushes up the hem of my dress, so it rests up around my hips. He looks down at my black thong like it's the most beautiful thing he's ever seen. "So beautiful," he praises reverently.

I pull at my wrists as the tape digs into my skin. I twist them back and forth with no progress. My pulse roars in my throat.

Pierce glides his hands up my thighs and grabs at my hips. He leans in and drags his nose up the column of my neck.

"Please, stop."

I'm helpless. I can't move. I can't fight him off.

Pierce has always made me uncomfortable. I didn't think he'd go this far, but I shouldn't be surprised. He's absolutely insane, just like Anthony.

My gaze wanders over his shoulder and connects with Dahlia. My tears don't blur her face. Her eyes are firm, and her muscles clenched. The stillness of her aura infuses me with the strength I need to endure. There's literally nothing I can do to stop what's going to happen. All I can do is accept it and keep going.

Pierce's hands continue to grope me, and my concentration on Dahlia doesn't waiver.

"Look away, Asher." My voice is hollow.

Asher's furious glower stabs at the side of Pierce's skill. "I'm going to kill you, you bastard! You hear me?! You're dead! A fucking dead man!"

I force away the feeling of Pierce's touch. It's like Novocain spreads with each stroke Pierce grazes across my skin.

My head turns to Asher. "Big guy." He stills. "Look away."

His eyes grow soft, and helplessness leaches into his body. "I'll never leave you, Princess." Asher's warmth seeps into my heart.

I'm not alone this time.

Shots sound from outside. Gunshots.

Pierce pulls away from me. "What the fuck?"

The glass of the windows shatters, and I take advantage of the opportunity. I thrust my head forward, and the crown of my head connects with his nose. He falls backwards as my chair tips towards him. I tumble on top of him and land as an "oomph" is pushed out of my gut.

"You broke my nose, bitch!" Pierce covers the middle of his face with his hand and blood escapes the cage made by his fingers.

There's a thunderous bang against the door.

"Shit!" Pierce pushes me off him and stands. The chair lands on its side, and my head thumps against the ground. Pierce pulls a gun from the waistband of his slacks and scowls at Asher, who's smiling like a loon.

"Who's out there?" Pierce shouts.

Asher's smile is permanent. "Who do you think?"

Pierce lets out an angry growl, then stomps to Asher and punches his cheek. Asher's head flies backward but bobs forward again. Pierce leans in and leaves Asher with a promise. "You can't keep her from me forever. I will come for her."

He turns and flees the warehouse through a door at the back.

The metal door at the front bursts open and in charges Rio, Zane, and . . . Is that Hayes? What the hell is he doing here?

"Took you long enough," Asher coughs out.

"I'd say we're right on time." Rio's casual tone is contradicted by the way he rushes over to Asher and begins the process of getting him down.

Hayes stands in shock, staring at Dahlia's half-naked body and the dried blood on her inner thighs.

"Hayes!" Zane snaps while sprinting to my side. "Get her down! We don't have much time. I'm sure backup will be here any minute."

Zane assesses my injuries and my exposed breasts. His jaw hardens, and a baleful glint enters his eyes. A whimper crawls up my throat.

"I tried, I promise. I tried to fight him off."

Zane trails the back of his finger down my cheek. He quickly removes his shirt and uses it to cover my chest. "Shhh. You did good, Angel. Nothing could make me stop loving you." Then he pulls out a switchblade and makes quick work of cutting the tape tethering me to the chair.

Tears swim in my eyes. "Now you tell me?"

"I've told you before. You just weren't listening."

When I'm free, Zane helps me into his shirt. He gathers me, one arm under my knees and one around my back and turns. We find that Hayes has Dahlia in his arms as well. He pulled up her pants, and her head rests on his shoulder. He whispers soothing words into her hair that calm the shaking of her body. Asher is standing with an arm around Rio, who carries most of his weight.

"We ready?" Zane asks Rio and Hayes. They both nod in return. "Ash, can you hold a gun?"

"Always," he answers, as if insulted.

Zane hands over a gun he pulled out from the back of his pants. "You two go out first." He nods to Asher and Rio. "Hayes and Iris in the middle, and Spencer and I will take up the rear."

We file out of the warehouse, leaving behind the horrors but taking a few ghosts with us.

CHAPTER 6

RIO

Asher weighs a fuck ton, but I still manage to carry most of his weight. I hold him on my left side so my shooting hand can be free in case I need to use my gun as we sidestep pools of blood and dead bodies.

The sun is high and beats down on my back. We're in the middle of White Plains, surrounded by more rundown warehouses with peeling paint and rust. Pavement and gravel crunch under our feet.

Fighting our way in here was almost too easy—there were only eight men outside armed with AR-15s and AK-47s. We took the subway as far as we could and then caught a cab but had the driver drop us off a mile away. We didn't find any security cameras, only a couple of men on the roof—they were the first to go. I used my knife to slit the first one's throat, and Zane did the same to the other, but his gun fell and alerted the rest of them to our presence.

The shootout didn't last long. Again, it was all easier than I thought it would be. It's like the men weren't even trying to actually hit us. Anthony should probably train his people before putting them to work.

"How are we going to get all of us out of here?" Asher pants.

"We're going to need a ride," I answer.

Asher gawks. "Seriously? You came here without an exit plan?"

"I'm not that dumb." I nod my head, gesturing to the black SUV in front of us.

"We're going to steal one of their cars? Are you sure you've thought this through?"

I scoff. "Of course, I have. *No soy estúpido*. It's not like they don't know where we live, or where we're going. They can come get their car if they want to." *I'm not stupid.* We approach the driver's side rear door only to find it locked.

"What now, Einstein?"

I lift the butt of my gun and smash the window in. Glass rains down on the pavement and I reach my hand into the shattered window, careful to avoid shards of glass, and unlock the door.

With a flourish, I open the door and gesture for Asher to get in. "After you, my liege."

Asher rolls his eyes and motions to step up into the car, but he falters. I'm right there to catch him, but I feel my heart stop. I don't want to alarm anyone, but Asher doesn't look good. The bullet wound in his shoulder needs to be treated. He's lost so much blood.

I swipe the glass onto the floor, not even registering the small pricks in my arm when the shards of glass pierce my skin. "*Vamos, viejo.* Let's get you in," I grunt as I help lift Asher in. *Come on, old man.*

He glares once he's settled in his seat. "I'm not that much older than you."

I only smile as I close the door in his face. Peering into the back of the SUV, I see that Hayes has made himself comfortable in the back, with Iris in his lap. He strokes her hair softly and whispers encouraging reassurances in her ear. Zane got Spencer situated in the seat next to Asher and is fiddling around under the steering wheel, likely trying to hotwire the car.

Opening the passenger door, I hop in the car and buckle my seatbelt. "Click it or ticket, *mis amigos,*" I shout backwards. *My friends.*

The roar of the engine fills my ears, and Zane sits up in his seat. He throws the car into drive, and the tires squeal as he speeds away.

"Asher needs a doctor," I whisper under my breath.

"Where do you think I'm heading?" Zane's voice has an edge to it, and I don't blame him. What we walked in on was worse than what I imagined. I knew it would be bad—I know how these things go—but there's a reason they say seeing and believing are two different things.

Anthony is going to die a slow death for what he did to them. With the way Iris's pants hung down around her legs and the dried blood on her inner thighs, it's not hard to guess what happened to her. Asher's bruises were expected but still alarming. I know he's tough, but that doesn't mean I want his limits to be tested. Then I saw Spencer, her ripped dress, and the black tear streaks that stained her cheeks . . .

Yeah, Anthony is fucking dead.

I turn my head back to check on everyone. Asher is lying across the seat with his head in Spencer's lap. His eyes are closed, but he speaks in a hushed voice that only Spencer can hear. She runs her hands through his hair and talks with him in the same tone.

I hate knowing that they went through . . . whatever that

fucker put them through. But I'm happy they had each other in that hellhole.

WE PULL up to the emergency room doors of St. Barnabas Hospital. The tame, brown brick building is in complete contrast with the chaos inside.

Zane throws the car into park, and we hop out together. "Are you sure Elena is on shift?"

"She basically lives here. If she's not, she's probably inside somewhere."

As we gather Spencer and Asher from the backseat, Hayes gets out of the back with Iris still in his arms. Zane runs inside and comes back out, followed by nurses and doctors with gurneys. They quickly get Asher loaded onto one and Spencer on another. They shout rapid-fire questions, asking about their condition and what's wrong. We answer each one as best we can.

Iris fights the doctor who is attempting to load her on a bed. She clings to Hayes's neck, refusing to release him or go anywhere without him.

"No! Don't touch me!" Iris kicks at the closest doctor.

Elena appears at the door, and her eyes widen in shock. She dashes toward us. "Stop it!" she yells as she pulls on the shoulder of the male doctor who has a hold of Iris's ankle. "What the hell is wrong with you?" She doesn't give him a chance to respond. "Inside, now! Go make your rounds."

Iris cries and Hayes keeps his arms firmly around her. "It's okay. It's okay," he tells her.

Elena places a hand on Hayes's shoulder. "If you wouldn't

mind coming with me, I can get her checked out inside. Are you okay to keep carrying her?"

Hayes nods and follows Elena inside.

The other nurses and doctors follow after Elena and head inside with Spencer and Asher. Zane and I follow suit and split when Spencer is taken to one room and Asher another. Zane tilts his head, gesturing to Spencer's door, then walks into Asher's room.

The swift beat of my heart settles as I walk through the door and spot Spencer lying in the hospital bed. Nurses and doctors hover over her, aiding with preliminary examinations and taking her vitals. She's a mess, but knowing she's here and that she's going to be okay makes me feel at ease.

Fucking finally.

After the staff assesses Spencer and determines she's not in critical condition, most of them clear the room except for one nurse and one doctor.

A *male* doctor.

Yeah, that's not fucking happening.

Before he can even introduce himself, I jump in. "I'd much rather Dr. Flores tend to her."

He looks to be not much older than me. He has pale skin with dark blond hair, and when his beady eyes turn on me, I can feel his ego bruise. "That's not up to you."

Spencer chimes in quickly. "Is Dr. Flores available?"

His displeasure turns to Spencer. "I'm perfectly capable of being your doctor, Ms . . ."

"Gray. Spencer Gray." Spencer bites her lip. "I'm sure you are, but I think . . . Umm . . ."

The nurse steps between Spencer and the doctor. "Doctor, why don't we let them be for a minute. The patient is stabilized, and I'm sure you have others you need to check in on."

The understanding nurse, in her bright pink scrubs, holds

her ground. Her words are polite, but her hands on her hips, wide-set feet, and firm voice suggest she's not going to budge on this. She's older and has dark brown hair with streaks of gray. She's short but still able to stare down a man a foot taller than her. Her ID reads "Amy Evans."

Amy leads the prick out of the light-stained wooden door but turns to us before she leaves. "I'll find Dr. Flores for you."

Once they're gone, I scooch my chair right next to Spencer. There's a hospital gown on the end of the bed. I pick it up and stand, holding my hand out to her. "Let's get you cleaned up, Mama."

Spencer lifts her hand to put it in mine, but she hesitates. It's enough to tear at my cool façade. I'm ready to drop to my knees and beg her to let me help her when she places her hand in mine.

Everything feels right when I'm touching her. All I need is her touch, and I know everything will be okay—everything will work out.

I help Spencer off the gurney and lead her to the bathroom. We stand on the plain gray tile together as Spencer shifts her weight from side to side.

Spencer's arms are crossed, and she won't look me in the eye as she says, "I've got it. Thank you."

She grabs for the gown, but I hold it just out of reach. "I'd like to look you over myself."

Swallowing a couple of times, she relents. "Okay, but don't stare." Spencer struggles to take off Zane's shirt, but once she gets it, and her dress, off, I'm frozen. Her torso is littered with black and blue bruises.

My veins grow hot as I hold out the thin aqua gown for Spencer to step into. My touch is gentle, but my hands tremble.

They're dead. They're all fucking dead.

CHAPTER 7

SPENCER

The beep of the heart monitor is muted in my ears. I'm covered in sheets and blankets, but I still feel cold.

I have an IV in one arm and a blood pressure cuff around the other. The fierce nurse came back about ten minutes ago and hooked me up to everything. She was efficient, but her touch was compassionate. Her nurturing nature reminded me of Texas.

It's the perfect taste of home, and I need that right now.

Guilt is shadowing my every move, waiting to swallow me whole. I know Rio sees my small flinches and my withdrawal—it has to be killing him—but I can't stop this destructive cycle in my head.

I want his touch and am happy he's here, but as he's about to give me what I want and touch me, the last few days flash in my head. Unable to control my reactions, I hesitate or flinch. Then guilt encroaches from the corner of the room, and my chest feels heavy. After which, I find myself back at step one.

Rio washed the makeup from my face after he dressed me

in the gown and did up the ties in the back. As I struggled with the ugly cycle of remorse, he was patient. It's like he saw every step and knew exactly what to do as I went through each one.

When I'd shy away, he would stop and take a step back. But once he saw the longing in my eyes, he would resume wiping away the dried mascara on my cheeks.

Even now, he sits next to my bed with his hand on my thigh. And when those memories enter the forefront of my consciousness, he removes his hand and rests it on the bed next to me. He waits for my yearning to build, then gives me what I need: his calming, comforting presence.

A low creak alerts me to the opening of the door. Elena is slow in her movements, entering the room as if she's approaching a feral animal, but her face is bright and open.

"Hey, Spencer!" She carries a clipboard with a light manilla file and gives it a quick glance. "Your vitals look good—great blood pressure, great heart rate. You were severely dehydrated, but the saline we have you hooked up to should help with that."

Rio stands, interrupting Elena. "What? *¿Ni un hola a tu hermano mayor?" No hello for your big brother?*

Elena gives Rio an annoyed look. "Hi, Rio." Her attitude flips as she switches back to me. "How are you feeling?"

Taking all the sunshine I can get, I crack a smile at their interaction. "Good. A little hungry, but good."

"That's great to hear. If you're okay with it, I need to ask you some tough questions, so I know how best to treat you." Elena becomes more serious.

Unsure of what to share, I glance at Rio. He nods, giving me the green light. Anticipating her questions, I preemptively give her some answers. "I have some bruising across my ribs." Mindlessly, my hand drifts over my torso. "I haven't eaten or had anything to drink in a few days, and I'm really tired."

Elena's scrutinizing gaze makes me feel bare. I stop myself

from covering my chest with my blanket. She doesn't ask the questions swirling around in her brain. Instead, she nods and sticks by her Hippocratic oath by providing me with the care I need.

She jots things down on her clipboard as she responds. "I can have some food sent in from the cafeteria. Amy will bring you some water. I want you peeing like a racehorse before you leave." She sets down the clipboard and steps up to the side of the bed opposite Rio. "May I feel your ribs? It's not going to be pleasant."

I nod my consent. She lifts my gown so it rests just under my breasts, but she makes sure I'm still modest by keeping my lower half covered with the blanket. She examines the bruises painted across my skin.

Her first touch is tentative, yet sure. The pain that shoots through my body causes me to gasp. I grapple to take a breath.

"You're hurting her!"

"Sit down, Rio. You know how this goes; you've broken your ribs more times than I can count. So, sit down." I'm not sure if it's Doctor Flores talking to him, his sibling Elena, or a mixture of both.

How many times has Rio broken his ribs?

Elena lowers my gown and gets me situated. "I want to do an X-ray to make sure nothing is broken. It doesn't look like it, but I don't want there to be any doubt."

"Okay," I agree, panting.

"I'll send in the tech ASAP, and—"

"*Female* tech," Rio interjects.

Elena gives Rio a flat look. "Yes, I'll send in a female tech for the X-ray. I'll look over the results and be back after. I'd feel better if you were to stay the night so we can observe you and make sure nothing else is wrong."

"No," I reply too forcefully.

Elena frowns. "Well, we'll see how you feel later." She spins on her heel and leaves.

I don't like the idea of staying here overnight. Anthony can find me again. He'll always find me.

"Mama, breathe." Rio is cupping my cheeks and leaning over my bed. The heart monitor beeps come too quickly. "Breathe with me." He mimics breathing in and out by dramatically lifting his shoulders then slouching.

"Sorry," I get out after a few breaths.

"No need to apologize, Baby Girl." His smile is sad as he wipes the tears I didn't know were falling, then sits back in his seat next to me.

I can't be this anxious mess—not now. This isn't the time to break.

I grab the fear that sits in the wings of my mind and shove it into a box. I lock the lid and throw it back into the black abyss. There, my fear will remain.

Until you can't hide it anymore . . .

CHAPTER 8

ZANE

The itch under my skin is unbearable. The LED lights are shining too bright, and the chatter of the nurses in the room is too loud. I want to dart out the door, run across the hall, and straight into the arms of the most beautiful woman I've ever known. My mind won't settle until I'm with her.

"Fuck!" Asher shouts and clenches his fists.

He's sitting on the bed, dressed in a hospital gown and hooked up to a saline IV. The paper-thin material barely fits him as it stretches across his wide shoulders, and the hem hits him at his upper thigh. I deftly lift my phone and snap a picture for Rio and Spencer to laugh at later.

Amy shakes her head. "Oh, hush. I need to finish cleaning the wound so I can stitch you up." She returns to cleaning Asher's gunshot wound. The kind, older nurse's patience knows no bounds. Asher has called her every name in the book, and every time, she ignores him and continues her work.

Elena has been in the room, enjoying the show. Even now,

she stares down at Asher's file in her hands, holding back a laugh.

We've already been over all of Asher's injuries. He has a couple of broken ribs, lacerations to his face and torso, bruising over most of his body, and, lastly, the bullet in his shoulder. He insists that he's fine, but when we first got here, the asshole doctor from earlier told us that Asher was suffering from blood loss and dehydration.

What a marvel observation.

Asher kicked him out within minutes and asked for Elena. As if she were waiting right outside the door, she walked in immediately. The asshole looked down his obnoxiously ugly nose at her, but like the champ Elena is, she ignored him and went right into doctor mode.

She removed the bullet from Asher's shoulder quickly and efficiently. Thankfully, nothing major was hit or damaged.

Nurse Amy begins sewing the hole in Asher's shoulder.

Asher hisses, "Holy shit."

Amy raises a brow. "For a large man with all those tattoos, you sure are a little baby."

"He doesn't like stitches," I mock-whisper to her.

"Shut up, dickwad," Asher shoots at me with a glower.

Amy and I chuckle together, and Elena covers her mouth with her hand.

"Are you even qualified to do this?" Asher gripes.

Elena steps up for her nurse. "Of course she is, you dick-wad. She's an APRN. I know you don't know what that means, so just trust me and stop being a whiny baby."

"Fine," Asher concedes.

Elena goes back into doctor mode. "I doubt you'll stay overnight for observation, even though your doctor, that's me, the one with the medical degree"—she points to herself—"is advising you to do so." She turns to me. "So, Z, you get to wear the nurse hat for the night."

"Don't bother asking for a sponge bath. Not going to happen," I grumble.

Asher grunts instead of responding. He grits his teeth as Amy continues her suturing.

Elena ignores my ribbing of Asher. "His ribs have hairline fractures, which is better than the alternative considering the potential for them to cave in and puncture his lungs after the beating he took."

Asher rolls his eyes. "Those pussies could barely throw a punch. I'm surprised they broke something."

Elena gives him a challenging look. "You're not twenty anymore, Ash. You can break a lot easier than fifteen years ago."

Complaining under his breath, Asher shifts back and forth on the bed.

Returning her attention to me, Elena continues. "Make sure he doesn't overdo it. If he gets hit in the ribs again, his lungs, or another vital organ, could get punctured."

I nod my head, knowing she won't let us leave until I listen to her whole speech.

"Antibiotic ointment can be applied to all of his cuts, and arnica cream will help with the bruising. His stitches can't get wet, so baths are probably best for now."

We've done this song and dance many times in the past. Even before Elena was in her residency here, she was always the one to put us back together. The number of wounds she has seen us with should be embarrassing.

The first time we came to her after we killed that guy in college, she didn't blink. The only thing that's changed is that she doesn't ask us questions anymore. Which is probably good considering we've never answered anyway. We don't want her to have to choose between the truth and lying for us in case we're ever caught.

Once Amy is done, and Elena has finished giving me her instructions, they both leave the room to get us discharge papers.

"I called off the manhunt for you and Spencer, and I had to pull some serious strings to keep the FBI and NYPD from rushing through the ER doors and demanding statements from you and Spencer," I inform him.

"Thanks for doing that." He sighs. "The last thing I need is to answer questions that I don't know how to answer right now." Asher closes his eyes, but there's more we need to discuss.

"You're going to have to talk about it, you know."

Asher swings his gaze to me. The turmoil in his eyes disappears as he speaks. "I'm fine. But we need to talk about Iris. She—"

"Iris can wait. We need to talk about what you went through, what *Spencer* went through," I interrupt.

Asher shakes his head. "No, I need to tell you—"

"We'll get to Iris, and why she was there, but the therapist Paloma made us all see after Rachel died said that we have to talk to each other—we have to get it out. We can't let that shit fester."

"Shut up about the damn therapist!" Asher erupts.

My eyes go wide. Out of the three of us, Asher is the one who has the hardest time sharing his feelings, but he usually does it.

Asher takes a deep breath. "Iris isn't who she says she is."

My brows scrunch together. "What are you talking about?"

"Did you do a background check on her?"

"Of course I did. But there weren't any red flags, so I didn't dig further."

Asher sighs. "That means Anthony knows someone, or paid someone to make her alias rock solid."

"Alias? Ash, what's going on?"

Asher gives me a concerned look. "Iris isn't her real name. It's Dahlia."

"What!"

CHAPTER 9

SPENCER

The drive back to my apartment is quiet. I shouldn't expect anything else, but that doesn't make the ride any less uncomfortable. We're in the same SUV we stole, and everyone is in the same spots as before, but this time, Asher sits upright, with one arm around me and the other in a sling. This type of contact between us is new but somehow familiar.

One of the nurses was able to find a pair of scrubs for Asher and me, which was a miracle. I don't know how Asher finds clothes that fit him.

Asher, Rio, and Zane all have their heads on a swivel, watching the traffic around us. We're safe, but the tension is as thick as the heavy humidity outside.

"So how 'bout them Astros?" I ask with a nervous chuckle.

Solid icebreaker. Good job.

Rio laughs from the passenger seat. "You're in New York, remember? It's the Yankees."

Hayes perks up in the backseat. "You're from Houston?"

Asher and Zane tense and my stomach hollows. I never told

Hayes, or anyone else at the studio, where I'm from. Not even Iris—Dahlia.

Maybe she already knew.

When no one answers, Hayes turns to Dahlia. "Did you know?"

She bites her lip and looks out the window.

"Iris?" Hayes urges.

"You probably shouldn't call her that, man," Zane proclaims from the driver's seat.

"Zane," I chastise, hoping to shut him up.

How does he know? Did Asher tell him?

"What are you talking about? Why not?" Hayes asks with an irritated frown.

Zane lets out a forceful laugh. "I'm saying you should ask your little girlfriend-slash-spy what her real name is."

Shit. This isn't good.

"Z," Asher warns, "stop it. We said we'd talk about this at Spencer's apartment."

"Spy?" Hayes questions as his head flinches back slightly.

Zane spews venom from the front of the car. "Tell him, *Dahlia.* Tell him who kept tabs on Spencer for months. Tell him why you were there."

Dahlia gasps, and her eyes widen.

"What?" Hayes asks, bewildered.

Leaning forward, I place a hand on his arm. "Zane, stop. It's okay."

Zane gives me a quick glance over his shoulder. "She's been feeding him information, Spencer. She's been his little spy from the beginning." His words remind me of the stinging betrayal I felt when Anthony first revealed who Dahlia was. But then the images of what happened next cause my heart to ache.

Hayes raises his voice. "Whose little spy?" We all ignore him and continue with our conversation in the front seat.

"She had to, Zane. If I were in her shoes, I would have done the same thing," I defend.

Zane's jaw clenches. "I know her reasons, but that doesn't mean I have to be okay with her choices."

My body tenses, and my blood boils. "I don't care what that sadistic bastard made her do! She's just as much a victim in this as I am! Same as all those kidnapped women that Anthony hurts!"

"Spencer . . ." Rio interjects. His eyes are soft and worried.

Asher brings his arm back around me and pulls me into his chest. The warmth from his body seeps into my bones. He clutches me tighter to him to get my body to stop trembling. "Let's finish this conversation when we get there."

Zane eyes me in the rearview mirror. His face is apologetic. I know he didn't mean to hurt me, but he wants to blame someone for what happened to us.

We all do.

And the person to blame will get what's coming to them. I'll make sure of it.

Zane parks unapologetically and illegally in front of my building, and he and Rio exit the car, scanning the street. They help Asher and me out of the back seat.

I inspect the windows of Abstract Dreams and Clay Creations. The lights are off, the stools are on the worktables in the studio, and all the art sits untouched in the gallery. Things look normal—nothing has changed, but at the same time, everything has changed. It's an odd feeling.

Asher holds his gun in his free hand and walks closely

behind me as we all make our way up my stairs with Hayes and Dahlia in the middle and Rio and Zane in the front.

"Wait here while we clear the apartment," Zane instructs, then opens my door with a key I definitely did not give him.

He catches my puzzled look and answers with a shrug. "I needed a way to get it inside in case you needed me."

"So, you stole my spare key?"

He smirks. "Sure—that's what I did."

If he didn't steal my spare, then where did he . . .

"You're thinking a little hard over there, Princess." Asher winks.

"Between the two of us, someone needs to," I quip and cross my arms.

A few minutes later, Rio pokes his head out of the open doorway. "Clear. Just be prepared, Mama."

My eyebrows squish together as I take a few steps forward. I should have heeded Rio's advice. My apartment is destroyed. All the kitchen cabinets are open, with their contents strewn about the tile. My TV is smashed to bits, and the cushions on my perfect couch are ripped apart—the white, wiry stuffing lies all over the floor.

I walk through the chaos straight to my room and find my clothing ripped to shreds. The fabric leaves a trail from my closet to my bed to the bathroom. My bed is torn apart just like my couch. Tears line my lashes as I take in the destruction all around me.

They're only things. Things can be replaced.

I breathe in for four, allowing my feelings in the moment to consume me.

Grief, loss, pain.

Then, I breathe out for four, letting go of the mindset that holds me back.

But it's not that simple, is it?

Because you need to talk about what happened.

A pair of tattooed hands land on my shoulders. "It'll be okay, Mama. We'll get it cleaned up and everything replaced."

I bite my lip, unable to form a response and nod my head. He wraps his arms around me and holds on tight.

Inhaling and exhaling shakily, I grasp onto his forearms to ground myself. He delicately places a kiss on the top of my head, and I lean back into his strength.

That's where Zane and Asher find us, not much later. They silently enter and offer me their comfort. Zane stands next to me and takes my left hand in his, lacing our fingers together. Asher places himself right in front of me and follows Zane's lead, grabbing my other hand. He leans his head down and rests his forehead against mine.

"We're here, Princess. We'll always be here."

Giving him a wobbly smile, I reply, "Stop calling me that."

His smile is full of male satisfaction. "You love it."

CHAPTER 10

SPENCER

It doesn't take as long as I anticipate to clean my apartment. Everyone, including Hayes and Dahlia, pitched in. Hayes left to take the trash down to the dumpster with Rio and Zane—they had to make a couple of trips and took the couch and bed as well.

And by "trash," I mean the life I've built here.

They're only things. Things can be replaced.

Speaking of which, Rio ordered a new bed and couch, Asher said he would take care of my dishes and other kitchen items, and Zane said he would restock my wardrobe. I gave him a skeptical look, but then he reminded me of the clothes he had stocked for me at their brownstone. I think I can trust him to get me the things I need and like.

The guys ordered pizza for all of us, and I pulled out extra pillows and blankets that remained untouched in the hall closet.

Looks like we're having a big sleepover.

Asher is doing another sweep across the floor with the broom to make sure we didn't miss any glass, and Hayes, Rio, and Zane return almost as quickly as they left with the last haul.

"Who is Dahlia?" Hayes questions.

Dahlia, who was standing at the window, tightens her shoulders.

"Hayes," I reprove, jumping up from my stool at the breakfast bar.

"No. I've been patient—I haven't pushed about any of it. But I walked into that warehouse too, so I deserve to know, who the hell is Dahlia?"

"I don't know if now is—" I start.

"Me," Dahlia interrupts, facing Hayes with her arms crossed over her torso. "I'm Dahlia."

Hayes rubs his forehead. "But your name is . . ."

"Dahlia." She braces as she waits for Hayes to react.

Hayes runs his hands through his hair, mussing it in the process. "Okay. Okay. Your name is Dahlia. So what?"

"Hayes." Zane places a hand on Hayes's shoulder. "There's more to it."

Stepping forward, I offer my support. "Dahlia, you don't have to do this." I make my way to her across the floor and grab her hand. Her eyes lock with mine and she breathes deeply, willing her tears to stay put.

Her lower lip trembles. "Why are you being so nice to me? You should be angry with me. You should hate me."

Smiling, I give her hand a squeeze. "You can't get rid of me that easily, babe. You're still my best bitch." I raise my hand and tuck some of her hair behind her ear.

She gives me a half-hearted smile. "Thank you."

"You don't have to do this right now, it can wait. You don't owe anyone answers."

"No, I can do this." She pats my hand and steps around

me. "My name is Dahlia Monroe. I was kidnapped from LA when I was sixteen."

Over the next bit, Dahlia spills her story—the same story she gave me in the warehouse. She recites the tale as if it happened to someone else, and I don't blame her. I'm sure the last few years of her life have been one terrible nightmare. While she's talking, Hayes moves to Dahlia's side. His gaze remains sympathetic.

When she's done, she lets out a breath.

Hayes stares at the floor, trying to make sense of everything he just learned. "So, the Bride Butcher is Spencer's ex—this Anthony dude."

Dahlia nods.

Hayes turns to me. "And he's killing women who look like you and dressing them in your wedding dress?"

I sigh. "Yeah."

Hayes rubs his chin. "What's up with the hyacinths?"

"He used to buy me those flowers after we'd fight. He said they showed how sorry he was."

Hayes's lip curls. "That's fucked up."

Dahlia pulls her hands away from Hayes and fidgets.

"Tell him," Asher pushes.

I give him a look that says *cut it out.*

He ignores me. "Hayes deserves to know the biggest part."

"There's more?" Hayes rapidly blinks.

Dahlia clears her throat. "Anthony, Spencer's ex, was able to keep me in line because he has my son."

Hayes's mouth falls open. "What?"

Tears finally fall from Dahlia's eyes. "He has my son."

Hayes grasps both of her hands in his. "You have a son?"

She nods again.

"We'll get him back." Hayes turns to Asher, Rio, and Zane. "We can get him back, right?"

"Of course," I answer. "We'll find him." I look to my men. Their doubtful gazes make my heart sink.

"We'll try," Rio promises.

Dahlia finally falls into a fit of hysterics. Her knees give out, but Hayes is there to catch her. As she sobs, she repeats over and over, "Thank you."

I can't imagine the weight she carries day to day, worrying about her son—not knowing if he's okay. No mother should have to go through that. That maternal instinct shouldn't be held over their head to control them.

Anthony's days of controlling Dahlia are over. I won't let him continue to hurt those I love.

It's time he meets the devil he helped create.

CHAPTER 11

ASHER

fter Spencer's declaration that we would save Dahlia's son, we ate Sal's pizza and sent Hayes and Dahlia to sleep in the guest room with enough pillows and blankets for an army. The now-destroyed guest bed probably would've been better on my back last week, but I couldn't ignore the overwhelming urge to stay between Spencer and any threats that may come through her front door.

Rio and Zane are down at the car, grabbing our bags. They were thoughtful enough to pack for us before they rescued us.

Thank God, because I would have hated to wear these stiff scrubs for another day.

With her ass in the air, Spencer finishes fluffing the pillows she laid out on her bedroom floor, forming a massive bed. If I didn't know any better, I'd think she was having sleepovers every weekend.

Spencer catches me staring and smiles sheepishly back at me. "I don't know where exactly y'all want to sleep, but I figured we could . . ."

I saunter over to her. "As long as I'm next to you, I have no complaints." I help her to her feet, wrap my free arm around her, and pull her close. She gasps when she feels how hard I am against her lower stomach.

She blushes and pushes closer to me. "Being with you should be the last thing on my mind after everything we went through." Her voice is breathy.

"There's no right or wrong time to be with someone you care about."

She gives me a sassy smirk. "What makes you think I care?"

Tracing my hand down her back, I grasp her ass. Hard. "I know you do."

Spencer squirms and raises up on her toes, nipping at my jaw. She's lost in the moment, in the feel of our bodies together. A spark of awareness flashes in her eyes as she groans in frustration and attempts to pull away. "Maybe when our friends aren't in the next room."

Leaning down, I nibble at her ear. "Then you need to quit rubbing that needy pussy all over my cock." She probably doesn't realize it, but she keeps moving her sex up and down my erect dick, making me impossibly hard in my pants.

Her moan is low. "Shit."

Ripping off the cockblock of a sling, I throw it aside and ignore the pull of my stitches. The ache of my wound screams, but I shove it aside. I need both hands to take what I've been craving.

Alarm mars her features. "Asher! You're going to hurt yourself!"

"I'm sure I could make you come with one hand, Princess, but two would make you scream much louder for me."

When she bites her lip and peers up at me through her lashes, I almost throw her down on the blankets and fuck her hard and fast. But I hold myself back, wanting to wring every drop of pleasure from that sweet as fuck body that has been teasing me from day one.

And with the way she's looking at me now? She wants me just as bad.

Falling to my knees, I lift her shirt and kiss my way across her stomach. I kiss each bruise, each testament of her strength, each shred of evidence of all she has endured. She hums as her hands tangle in my hair and remove the hair tie securing my bun.

My fingers slip into the top hem of her pants and slip them down her silky-smooth legs, along with her panties. With her hands on my shoulders, she steps out of her pants and stares down at me. The fire burning in her gaze causes my hands to shake.

With her eyes locked on mine, she removes her top, revealing that she isn't wearing a bra, but she covers her perfect breasts with her arm. My eyes drink in every curve, every bruise. I note each shiver as my eyes skim all the places I'm going to put my hands and my mouth.

I move a step towards her, but she holds up a hand, stopping me.

"Is it still a mistake?" Her question is whispered and tinged with insecurity.

That's my fault.

I placed those thoughts in her head. *I* needed them there because if she doubted me, then I was safe. I could keep my distance.

But I can't anymore. The distance was a fabrication of my mind. Since I met her, I haven't been able to go a single day without laying my eyes on her—on her soft curves and open heart.

"You could never be a mistake, Princess."

She finally drops her arm, exposing her peaked mauve

nipples. I close the distance between us, and my hands skirt the outer swell of each breast and skim down her abdomen. Goosebumps rise in the wake of my touch.

When my eyes land on her glistening sex my restraint is annihilated.

My hands grip her hips, my fingers digging into her flesh. She gasps, and her pupils dilate at the slight bite of pain.

Noted.

I throw Spencer down onto the mound of pillows and blankets she put together, and she yelps. Once again, I ignore the twinge in my shoulder. Scrambling on top of her, I cover her mouth.

"You need to keep quiet unless you want everyone to hear and know exactly what we're doing in here."

Her eyes flare with arousal.

"Then again, maybe that's exactly what you want." Removing my hand from silencing her, I trace her lips with my fingertip. Unable to resist anymore, I smash my lips to hers. She returns my passion with an electricity of her own. My tongue eagerly invades her mouth when she opens up to me, and she swallows my unbridled groan.

My hands coast down her arms, encircling her wrists. Without warning, I bring her hands up above her head, giving them a slight squeeze. She arches into me, her perfect breasts scraping against the fabric of my shirt. Spencer clenches her thighs at the sensation.

No, no, no. That won't do.

I need those luscious thighs wrapped tight around my waist.

"Stay," I command, releasing her wrists. I sit back on my knees and wrench her legs apart. I gape down at her bare, pink sex. The scent of her arousal fills my senses as I inhale deeply.

If any more blood goes to my cock, I'm going to pass out.

"You're killing me, Princess," I growl.

Spencer's cheeks pinken with humiliation, and she makes an attempt to close her legs.

That won't do either.

I hold her legs firmly, keeping her spread for my viewing pleasure. Glancing around the room, I search for anything to help keep her open for me. But I come up with nothing.

Next time.

Again, I give her the same command. "Stay."

She steadies herself with a long calming breath and closes her eyes.

"Eyes open, Baby. Always keep your eyes open and on me."

When she does as I say, I lie on my stomach and part her lower lips with my fingers. Only then do I finally allow myself to get my first taste of her, straight from the source. Spencer turns her head and bites her shoulder to muffle the scream.

Mmm . . . I don't think that will do either.

I want her screaming so loud the neighbors call the cops. I want her voice hoarse from shouting my name. I want her unleashed and bucking her hips so I choke on her sweet juices.

My tongue dances up and down her slit, tangling with her clit and circling her needy entrance. Her eyes remain on me as I play with her swollen core. The need to come builds and builds in her body as she writhes.

When I shove my tongue inside her, her inner muscles clench. I go in and out, simulating exactly what I want to do with my dick. It takes everything in me to keep from coming in my stiff scrubs, and I can't help but rock my hips into the ground.

Replacing my tongue with two of my digits, Spencer finally lets a husky moan free without smothering the sound. Wanting to hear that harmony on repeat, I thrust my fingers in and out of her pussy and attack her hooded clit with my tongue.

Spencer's hips create a rhythm with my hand as she chases

her release. I want her to find that complete loss of control, so I hook my fingers and find that ribbed spot inside her.

"Ash!"

Her climax is glorious. Her shout is strangled with pleasure, and her thighs clamp around my head as I continue to stroke her as she falls over the edge. She soaks the blanket below her with her cum.

There's no doubt in my mind that everyone on this entire city block knows what we're doing by now.

When her legs fall away from my head, I crawl up her body, whispering praises into her golden skin.

"Such a good girl, keeping your hands up."

She hums and smirks in blissful satisfaction, still embracing the high of her climax. "Don't get used to it, big guy. I may not be so obedient all the time."

"That's fine. I don't crave a mindless doll." Her eyes fly open and lock on me with skepticism. My hand circles her throat and slides down her chest. I finally get a handful of her full breast as I explain. "I crave your submission. I crave your trust."

With my free hand, I flick her other nipple. She gasps and thrusts her chest up in an erotic offering.

Don't mind if I do.

My mouth envelops her mound, dragging my tongue back and forth over the peak. Her hands dive into my hair again, mussing it up. I continue my ministrations then switch to the other side until she's a whimpering mess of need.

When I lift my head from her chest, she tugs at my shirt. "Take it off—I need it off. I need to feel you."

I smile and comply with her plea, sitting back on my haunches. Her hands graze down my chest and over my inked arms. I let her hands roam and feel every inch of my skin. As they coast down my eight-pack, my cock twitches.

She spots the motion and continues her path to the top of my pants.

"Please. Take these off. They need to come off."

Slipping my pants along with my boxers down my thighs, I stand and remove them in one sweep. Her eyes wander my body and take in every detail. She savors the view as I savor my own.

But when her knees bend and fall apart, inviting me to partake in what we both need, I rush back to her.

"Are you sure?"

I give her one last out. One last chance. Zane and Rio have both already fucked her, and once I get this taste of heaven, there's no going back.

Spencer will forever be ours.

Her hands trace the hair on my face and guide my mouth to hers. Her kiss is sure and full of lust. When she pulls back, she grants me the answer I hope for. "I've never been more sure of anything."

Thank God.

If she had said no, I would've died right here from a massive case of blue balls.

Lining my cock with her opening, I thrust forward. Something in my chest shatters, or maybe it's everything in my life finally sliding into place.

I grunt as I work my full length into her small hole. Even after an orgasm and all her cum, she's still tight as hell. Her hands fly to my ass and urge me inside her, so I slam home in one forceful drive.

The sting of the skin on my shoulder lets me know I've torn a stitch or two, but my affliction is easily ignored.

A garbled shout comes from Spencer as she adjusts to the fullness of my dick in her pussy. Her nails dig into my flesh, no doubt leaving behind crescent-shaped marks.

The stretch of her muscles around my shaft has me seeing stars. Her warm slick channel is enough to make any man go mad. The veins in my neck pop out as I attempt to reign in my control.

One time tonight isn't going to be enough.

Through clenched teeth, I inform her, "I'm not going to be able to be gentle, Princess. This is going to be rough and raw."

Her voice is gravelly. "I don't want gentle. I want you just as you are—rough, wild, intense. I want it all."

Blood trickles down my arm as I reach for her hand and bring it to my mouth, kissing her palm sweetly. Red marks her hand where I touched her.

Then I abruptly pull my hips back, retreating from her warmth, and thrust forward. Her hands wrap around me to my back as I piston my hips in and out of her pussy. She claws at my back, leaving behind more of her marks.

I revel in the pain she gives me. I know I'm giving her just as much as I brutally make my cunt mine.

Grasping her knees, I bring them to her chest and sit back. I shove my dick inside her again, the new angle brings us both a new level of bliss.

"You feel so good, Princess."

She reaches for me but only grasps onto my arms. Her chest heaves up and down as her breaths increase in tempo.

"Are you gonna come for me, right here in your bedroom, Princess? When someone could walk in the door any second and see how beautifully you take my cock."

Drops of crimson fall to her chest. I swirl my finger in them and paint my name across her chest, marking her as mine.

Her eyes follow the motions, and her inner muscles once again begin to spasm around me, letting me know she's close. So very close.

"Shit, shit, shit," she mutters.

I snake my hand between our bodies and flick her bundle of nerves—the blood on my fingertips makes the action even more deft. She screams her release as I find my own. Spencer's pussy milks my cock empty of every drop of cum. The buzzing in my ears subsides, and with one last squeeze of my cock, Spencer's body relaxes beneath mine.

My arms give out, but I catch myself on my elbows so as not to crush her. My shaft hardens again as I look down at the mess I made of her. She smiles up at me, sated and happy, with an afterglow of two orgasms.

I'm not sure how long she'll be smiling like that when I start up round two.

CHAPTER 12

SPENCER

We lay in a sated heap on the mess of blankets and pillows. My head rests on Asher's stomach while Rio and Zane cuddle each other behind me. They strolled in with our bags and smug, knowing looks on their faces after Asher finished cleaning me up from our few bouts of lovemaking. The comments Rio made about us *finally being done* were followed by *umphs* from Asher punching him in the gut.

That's right—bouts. Plural. As in, more than once!

But they said nothing and just helped Asher clean up the mess we made, replacing the ruined blankets and pillows with fresh ones.

Yes, I know I have an abnormal number of blankets. It is what it is.

Asher dressed in the bare minimum, while Zane and Rio stripped down to make themselves comfortable. Rio, Zane, and I all but held Asher down and made him put his sling back on after Zane fixed Asher's stitches. I'm not sure where he got the suture kit, but they won't catch me complaining.

I slipped on the only shirt within reach and the glee that took over Rio's face told me all I needed to know.

It's his.

Now we're all here, together, in this perfect moment. A moment untouched by the sad, tragic ugliness of the world.

An uncontrollable, satisfied smile graces my swollen lips, and Rio traces the curve with his finger. "*Esa es una hermosa vista. La podría ver todos los días.*"

Now, that's a beautiful sight. I could look at it all day.

A blush crawls up my cheeks, and I cover my face. Another hand grabs mine, and a beautiful face with a sharp jaw and emerald eyes swims into view.

"Don't hide from us, Angel."

My blush doubles and spreads across my chest.

Is it possible to die from swooning too much? I might be the first case and become a medical marvel.

Asher's hand runs through my hair, lulling me into a restful state, but the tension in his body causes me to look up. His brows are drawn together, and his lips are pursed in concentration as he stares up at the ceiling.

"Hey," I whisper, breaking his focus. "What's going on? I thought orgasms were supposed to relieve stress, not cause it." My teasing doesn't have the intended effect.

Without relaxing, he gives me a small, placating smile. "And I thought orgasms were supposed to get rid of your sass."

Rolling onto my stomach, I rest my hands and chin on his taut abs. "Guess we're both wrong."

He snorts out a laugh, but the clouds remain in his eyes.

"Talk to me," I implore as his gaze wanders to the side. I raise my hand and tousle his hair.

His half-hearted smile is like a dense weight on my chest. He reads the stress on my face. "It was something Anthony said."

Situation, meet a large bucket of ice.

Sweat breaks out across my back, and every muscle in my body strains. This is not where I thought this was going to go.

Zane sits up. "I think it's time we talk."

Never the words a girl wants to hear.

We all sit up, feeling the seriousness of Zane's statement. Asher narrows his eyes and pulls me onto his lap as he catches Rio's gleeful expression return. Rio retaliates by placing my feet in his lap.

"Sharing is caring, *amgio*," Rio jests with a wink.

"Enough, you two," Zane asserts. "We have to talk about what happened."

My heart pounds as the box I stored in the back of my mind jumps off the shelf. "I'm good. Thanks for the kumbaya."

I get my feet under me, ready to stand, but a set of colorful, tattooed arms and multiple hands keep me in place. The menacing glare I shoot each of them does zero favors for me.

Zane speaks first. "After our ex-girlfriend—"

"Rachel? You all dated her?" I interrupt.

Rio's head rears back. "How do you know about Rachel?"

"Anthony. While we were . . . *there* . . . he brought her up and rubbed her death in Asher's face." I mentally stomp on my box of nightmares, keeping the horrors inside.

"I see." Rio nods his head.

They don't owe me anything, but my curiosity gets the best of me. "What happened with Rachel?"

Asher rubs his hand over his mouth. "We met her when we were all at NYU. She was a sorority girl —the life of the party. When she set her sights on us, we fell under her spell instantly. But she was still seeing other people. One guy in particular was on the football team and didn't like that we caught him trying to roofie half the cheerleading team."

There's a special place in hell for men like that.

I grab Asher's hand as he struggles with the rest of his story.

"He wanted to get payback because we informed the school of what he was doing, and he was kicked off the team. So, he seduced Rachel into his bed. But instead of having a one-night stand with her, he tied her to a chair and recorded himself raping her. He posted the video on the internet with the title 'BDSM sorority whore.'"

Squeezing my eyes shut, I try to hide myself from the tragic story. No matter what kind of lifestyle Rachel lived, she didn't deserve that.

"She couldn't handle the bullying and ridicule that followed. We did our best to shield her from it, but I'm sure there was more we could have done. When I got back to my room after class one day, I found her in my closet. She had hung herself with my belt. After that, we found the football player and did what we do best."

"You killed him?" I ask for clarification.

"Yes, we did," Zane answers.

"Good."

Zane's features soften. I didn't realize he was nervous, anticipating my judgement. "After Rachel died, Paloma made us all see a therapist. She told us we need to talk to each other, especially considering we wouldn't confide in her. Now, when anything happens, we talk about it as soon as possible."

So, this is part of what keeps them together. This is part of their foundation. They're not those guys that stick together out of familiarity or proximity. Their bond is cemented into their souls because they've seen each other in the bad times. They've walked through the trenches together.

This isn't just friendship. It's family.

And they want me to be a part of it.

Water leaks from the corner of my eyes as the feeling of rightness takes hold of my heart. This is where I belong. This is where I want to be.

With them.

They let me have my moment as everything sinks in. Asher keeps his arms wrapped around my middle while Zane and Rio hold my hands.

"We need to talk about your mom," Asher states.

I freeze. "I don't think that's necessary. She said all she had to say."

"Yeah, but you didn't." Zane gestures to me.

Of course, Asher already told them about my mother's role in everything. Shaking my head in denial, I push the betrayal down into a dark abyss.

"Don't let it eat you alive. Don't let her win, Mama."

My body trembles as I hold in a scream of frustration. It doesn't last long, though.

I jump to my feet. "She didn't win! There's nothing to win! This isn't a game! This is my life! She fucked with *my life*!"

Asher, Rio, and Zane stand as well, monitoring my outburst.

"How could she do that to me? What kind of mother sells her child?" I pace back and forth over the bed of pillows and blankets.

Zane's tone is sincere. "No mother should ever do that. I'm so sorry she made that choice."

I throw my hands in the air. "You shouldn't be sorry! You didn't do anything wrong! She needs to be sorry. She *sold* me. She sold my virginity to the highest bidder, and she didn't care. All she saw when she looked at me were dollar signs."

"I know, Princess." Asher is calm.

They're all fucking calm . . .

How are they all so calm?

Whirling on them, I direct my frustration at them. "Why aren't you angrier about this? Any of you!"

None of them react.

"Oh, we're fuming, Angel. But we don't have the right to scream here, you do. She hurt *you*. She sold *you*. Not us."

Betrayal spreads through my heart. It's accompanied by grief, then fury.

"She has to pay—I have to make her pay for what she did." My voice cracks.

"We can help with that," Rio assures me.

With their support, I recount the rest of the details I can remember about the last few days, and the box with the perfectly fitted lid bursts open. I share every moment I thought I was about to watch Asher die, what it felt like when all those men took turns with Dahlia, and every minute I waited for the worst.

When I'm done, my hollow body bends, and I finally sit back down, surrounded by unconditional love. My eyes are swollen from expelled tears, but I feel lighter at the same time. Not once did they judge me. Not once did my men tell me to get over it.

My exhausted mind is ready for sleep, but I can't just give in just yet.

Then Asher takes his turn. My chest aches as he recounts watching Pierce coming close to assaulting me. I'm ripped apart when he admits to the fear he felt each second we were in Anthony's hands.

By the time Asher's done talking, the sun is coming up, my eyelids are heavy, and I'm sagging against Asher's chest. Rio is lying on his side with his head in Zane's lap, and Zane's face is calculating.

"Where's the list?"

I groan in Zane's direction. "How are you still so awake?"

Rio grumbles with his eyes closed. "Zane and Asher are like robots. They can stay awake by literally commanding their bodies to do so. It's like some freaky law enforcement gift."

A small chuckle slips out. "Were you not blessed with the same gift?"

"I think it's about time to put the children to bed," Asher teases.

Zane ignores us. "It wouldn't be a physical list. Something like that would degrade over time, so it's probably on a jump drive or something like that. We know he still hasn't found it, and he needs it back—he tore this place apart looking for it." He stands, causing Rio's head to jostle.

"*Ay dios mio*," Rio complains.

Zane paces the room. "I bet they've already torn apart the brownstone, but everything you brought there is in your . . ."

You've got to be fucking kidding me. He better not have . . .

Jumping out of Asher's arms, I sprint across the room to my duffle bag, which is currently resting by the front door. My men surround me as I dig through the bag until I find what I'm looking for. The cold of the ceramic freezes me.

"You son of a bitch. I swear if you—" Before I finish the thought, I remove the lid and reverently set it aside.

Zane shines a light from his phone inside Abuela's urn. A reflection from a small piece of silver metal shines in my eye. I reach my hand into the ashes of the person I miss the most and fish out a flash drive.

My body shakes involuntarily. Holding back an enraged scream, I push out through gritted teeth, "That motherfucker."

CHAPTER 13

ASHER

Spencer is ready to explode—her body is practically vibrating. If Spencer could set Anthony on fire with her mind, she would have summoned the fires of Hell by now.

Rio grabs the urn and replaces the lid, setting it aside, as Zane helps Spencer to her feet and slips the flash drive out of her hands. He digs his laptop out of his gym bag and gets to work at the breakfast bar. Spencer's nostrils flare as she breathes in and out.

I grab her by her upper arms and turn her to face me. "Hey, look at me." Her face turns to me, and the pure fury there promises pain. She's itching to bring down a world of agony on Anthony.

"He has to pay. He can't get away with this . . . Abuela's ashes! He put that damn list in her ashes!" Her voice gets louder and louder.

My hands move to her shoulders. "He will. We can make that happen."

Looking at Zane's screen, all I see are ones and zeroes as he types away on his computer.

"Holy shit. You guys need to see this." Zane waves us over. "This idiot had the USB encrypted, but he must have gone cheap when paying someone to do it for him. It was stupid easy to figure out."

We all surround him and look at the screen over his shoulder. The list has names, dates, and dollar amounts.

Rio reads, "Fifty thousand. Sixty-two thousand. Twenty-seven thousand."

"It's all of Anthony's sales," Spencer observes. She points at the screen. "Is that a New York senator right there?"

Zane scrolls through the list. "It looks like he's dealt with almost everyone in the country and then some. There are celebrities, A-listers, politicians—"

"The numbers next to the names are . . ." Spencer trails off as she mentally works out the answer to her question. "Prices?"

"Or more than one person," Rio adds absentmindedly.

Spencer grimaces. "Just when I thought I couldn't get any more disgusted."

A knob turns in the hallway, and Dahlia and Hayes walk out of Spencer's bedroom. Neither looks like they've slept much. Dahlia's hair is messy and not in the *I was just fucked into oblivion* kind of way. More like she probably tossed and turned all night. They both have dark bags under their eyes.

Hayes puts on a fake smile. "Good morning! Everyone sleep okay?"

Despite my exhaustion, I reply, saying, "Like babies."

"Speak for yourself," Spencer groans. She rounds the breakfast bar and goes straight to Dahlia. The two embrace, and a secret conversation passes between them. They pull apart with their arms still around each other. Dahlia takes a deep breath as Spencer whispers, "You got this, babe."

They both turn to all of us as Spencer says, "We need to find August."

Rio steps forward. "Who's August?"

"My son," Dahlia answers.

"Shit." Rio rubs the back of his neck and turns to Zane. "Do you have any CIs that might be able to give us something?"

"We can always try Hank again," Zane suggests, but his voice lacks confidence.

"I want to help," Spencer claims as she widens her stance, facing us.

"I think the fuck not!" Zane jumps up from his stool.

"¡Ni en un million años!" Not in a million years.

"Not a good idea, Princess," I protest. The three of us cross the room, standing before her with our arms folded. Any other person would be shitting their pants right now, but Spencer digs in her heels.

"I'm coming with you whether you like it or not." Her words are tinged with menace.

"Me too," Dahlia inserts with a determination that only a mother can muster.

Hayes's face looks like he swallowed something sour as he slides an arm around Dahlia's shoulders and adds his opinion to the lot. "Definitely not! We just got you two back, and now you want to turn right around and walk into the fire? Seriously? Hell no."

Dahlia stands strong. "August is my son—*my* son! Anthony has held him hostage for years! I'm going to be the one to get him out of there."

"Dahlia, I can't imagine what that's like, but it's not safe. Having you and Spencer there could be a distraction for us, putting everyone at greater risk. You and Spencer can't come," Zane says sympathetically but firmly.

Spencer throws her arms down at her sides, fists clenched. "I'm going!"

Rio is going to lose his cool. "*Sobre mi cadaver.*" *Over my dead body.*

"No," I bark out with grave deliberation.

"I will pull out the handcuffs if I have to," Zane threatens.

Spencer's cheeks flame, and she pulls her shoulders back. "Try it and see what happens. I took both of you the other day no problem."

Dahlia and Hayes chortle, and Spencer's cheeks flame in a whole different way now.

"Finally got your donut holes glazed, I see," Dahlia teases.

She stammers through her explanation with wild hand gestures. "Holy shit, that's not what I meant. It's just that . . . we were fighting and I tackled them. But it's not what you think."

Zane strokes his chin sarcastically. "Mmm, but it turned out to be exactly what everyone is thinking."

Spencer lets out a horrified gasp, and her eyes widen briefly. "Oh my God! Shut up!" She swats at Zane, but he catches her wrist and brings her close.

"Calm down, Angel. The fact remains; you're not tagging along." Zane turns to Dahlia. "And you're not tagging along." Then he turns to Hayes. "And *you're* not tagging along."

Hayes makes an offended face. "Hey now! What did I do? I more than proved how helpful I am yesterday."

Rio waves a hand at Hayes. "You did one thing, Superman —whoop-dee-doo. Sit down. The grownups are talking."

Hayes's voice is hard. "August is Iri—Dahlia's son. Dahlia is my girlfriend. Are you making the connections that I am? I'm fucking going."

Rio, Zane, and I all look at each other. Our eyes convey the skepticism we all share. If we leave them here, they'll probably follow us anyway. And if we bring them with us, they'll just get in the way.

This is going to be a shit show.

I clear my throat. "Fine. Let's discuss ground rules first." There are some complaints from Spencer, Dahlia, and Hayes as I tell them that they have to stay with us at all times, and that none of them are getting guns. But after Zane twirls his handcuffs around his fingers a few times, the three newbies keep the objections to themselves.

After groceries are delivered, I make breakfast for everyone, Rio runs to The Mudhouse for coffee, and Zane continues digging through Anthony's client list at the breakfast bar. Spencer and Dahlia went to the bathroom together—traveling in a pack like all women do when they go to the bathroom— and Hayes is standing guard at the window. No one asked him to, but I can understand his instinct to protect those he loves.

"Oh fuck. Asher!" Zane leans back and puts his hands on the back of his neck.

Finishing up the last of the scrambled eggs, I turn off the burner and walk behind Zane to get a look at his screen. "What's up?"

"I dug into his finances and found the transaction we were looking for. He definitely made the purchase."

My eyes flit across the screen, scouring for what he wants me to see. I lock on a single name and slam my hands down on the marble surface.

"That son of a bitch."

CHAPTER 14

SPENCER

Breathe. Aim. Bend. Release.

The knife embeds itself at the bottom of the target, nowhere near the bullseye. "Damnit."

Rio smirks next to me. "You're at least hitting the target. And it might help if you aim with both eyes open."

Giving him a deadpan glare, I cross my arms. "Very funny. Mr. Flores is full of jokes today."

Zane snickers on my other side. I attempt to give him the same look I gave to Rio, but when I lay my eyes on his profile, I fail. I melt into a puddle of goo as I trace the line of his jaw with my gaze. My pussy clenches, empty and begging to be filled, as I remember the other night on their living room floor.

Focus. Training, not banging.

Blinking away my horny haze, I clear my throat and turn back to the target. "Both eyes open. Got it."

Walking to retrieve my knife, I take in the warehouse one more time. When Rio, Asher, and Zane brought me, Dahlia, and Hayes here on Monday, I thought they had lost their minds. I don't know what it is with men who kill and warehouses—it must be a requirement. Is there a book on this shit?

Rule #1: If you want to kill people, you must own a warehouse.

The warehouse is a little smaller than . . . the only other warehouse I've ever been in. And thank God, this one is nothing like the first. The floors are concrete but clean, and there's more lighting that illuminates the space. Rows of metal shelves cover one-half of the warehouse, and the guys arranged the other half as a training space for me, Dahlia, and Hayes. Rio grabbed a couple of targets from somewhere amongst the sea of shelves. Asher and Zane had no idea where Rio got those, or when he even brought them here. When asked those questions, he answered with a shrug. "I'm like a Boy Scout—always prepared."

That first day was a mess. I thought I had a good aim, but that was proven wrong. My hand-to-hand combat skills passed my guys' inspection, but they said they didn't want me to have to rely on them because then that would mean that someone is too close. So, Rio insisted I learn how to use knives. That, too, was a disaster.

At least I'm hitting the target today.

Dahlia made a point to let us know she doesn't like violence. But when her self-defense and shooting were tested, she was a natural.

Hayes's skills with a gun were a shock. Rio and Zane put a Glock on the table in front of him and said, "Show us." He kept eye contact with Rio and Zane while he disassembled the gun completely, then reassembled it in under one minute.

The guys said that Dahlia and Hayes were good to go, but apparently, I still need help. Hence the useless target practice.

The guys have been taking me out, teaching me what they call "survival skills." We usually go to the warehouse or "The Bat Cave," as I have come to call it, and go over hand-to-hand combat, shooting, knife-throwing, or anything that could help me strike and get away.

Ripping the knife out of the wooden target, I return to my place ten feet away, between Rio and Zane.

Breathe. Aim. Bend. Release.

The knife lands in the second ring from the bullseye.

"Yes!" I exclaim, jumping up and down.

Rio lifts me up and spins me around. *"Bien hecho,* Mama!" *Well done.*

He sets me down and gives me a quick, passionate kiss, then passes me to Zane, who gives me a congratulatory hug and a kiss as well. I step back with a huge smile on my face.

The door squeaks open as Asher ambles in. He's wearing the sling, despite his constant complaining. None of us will let him take it off.

"Hey! You finally hit the target," Asher teases.

I shoot him a menacing glare. "Fuck off."

My swearing amuses him, which only makes me more flustered.

"We need to load up," Asher informs Rio and Zane. "I want us prepared in case anything happens. Anthony and Pierce have been too quiet lately."

"Good idea," Rio comments.

They all spread out amongst the various wood crates and metal shelves and begin to dig through them.

"Umm. What should I do?" I shuffle from foot to foot.

Zane tosses me a plain black duffle bag. "You heard Asher. Load up."

Asher puts his hand on the small of my back and leads me over to Rio and Zane. I feel that spark zip through me at his touch. Lord, these men have turned me into a very horny woman.

Not now, vagina. You need to learn timing.

Asher hands me a duffle bag and says, "Grab what you want—however much you want." I still have no idea where these bags are coming from.

"Words every woman wants to hear. Although I won't lie, I always imagined it would happen in a store on fifth." I laugh as I peer into the wooden crates.

Guns, ammo, zip ties, and grenades. All that and more.

"Noted," he says with a wink and starts to fill his own bag.

I wander from crate to shelf and back, checking out all their "supplies." I grab some handguns and the proper ammo, but this bag is getting heavier by the second. So much for working out, I can barely hold this dumb duffle bag.

"I got you." Rio appears next to me and takes the bag from my hands.

"Where's your bag?"

"I already grabbed everything I need," he says while looking me up and down appreciatively.

My face immediately heats, and I stumble over my words. "Oh. Well. That's good. That's important. To have what you need, I mean. When you need it."

He sets my bag down, tugs me by my waist, and brings my body flush with his. "I'll always have what I need because I'm never letting you go, Mama." I begin panting at his words and feel my heart beat rapidly. Staring into his eyes, I can see the fire—his need for me. I feel it wash over me.

"Rio? Spencer? Ready to go?" Zane calls out for us.

I break away from his gaze and sigh, looking around.

"Too bad we're leaving already. This place would be so fun to play hide-and-seek," I say with a fake pout and attempt to pull away, but Rio doesn't let go.

I look back and see that fire burning hotter. "You have no idea what you just started, Mama," he says with a wide, crazed smile.

"What are you talking about?"

"We enjoy the hunt, Spencer. Especially when we're together."

At his truth, my eyes widen. They would never hurt me—I know that. I'm safe with them. Always will be. I just never imagined that they felt that way.

"Hey, guys!" Rio calls for Asher and Zane.

Now I'm thoroughly confused. What is going on? Are we really going to play a child's game?

"What's up?" Asher questions as he and Zane round a metal shelf and come into view.

"Spencer, here, wants to play a little game," Rio says to them without looking away from me.

"I just said that it would be fun to play hide-and-seek. I always had fun playing it at friends' houses growing up and was really good at it," I defend myself. I don't want to seem young and childish.

I may be inexperienced. Or I *was* inexperienced.

Zane and Asher grin at each other and prowl forward, that same crazed fire burning in their eyes, matching Rio. Why do I feel like I walked into a viper's nest?

Rio slides his hands down to my ass and squeezes as Zane crowds me on the right, leaning down to trail his nose along the length of my neck. Asher stands to my left and grabs my chin firmly, angling my face to look at him.

"You gonna hide for us, Baby?"

"You mean hide *from* you," I corrected him.

"No. Hide *for* us," he says right before he smashes his lips to mine. I instantly open my mouth, and he takes full advantage of my submission, swiping his tongue into my mouth seductively.

My body is overwhelmed with sensation. Zane lightly bites my neck while his hands pull the V of my shirt lower. Once my bra is exposed, Rio comments, playfully, "Black lace? Mama, were you planning on seducing us?"

Maybe . . .

I pull away from Asher to refute Rio's claim, but he grabs my hair with one hand and pulls, forcing me to look back at him.

"You have sixty seconds to run and hide before we find you, and when we do, Rio is going to fuck that sweet pussy of yours and Zane is going to fuck your throat."

My pussy throbs and I swallow hard. I don't deny I want it —their touch. I'm desperate for it.

Instead, I ask, "What are *you* going to do if you find me?"

"*When* I find you, I get to fuck your tight little ass."

I gasp and my heart picks up speed. Do I want that? I've never done that before. I've heard women whisper about it. Some say it's fun. Some say it's miserable.

But my body still yearns for their touch and my panties are even more wet than they were before. I'd say it's safe to assume I want that too.

Rio leans down so he's right in my face. "Run."

They all let go at once, but I don't move. Shock, fear, excitement, and arousal all surge through me, leaving me paralyzed and speechless.

"One, two, three—" Rio begins to count. That snaps me out of my stupor, and I bolt. A quick glance behind me reveals Asher removing his sling and wearing a huge smile.

I didn't get a good look around when I was on my weapon shopping spree. So, I'm relying on instinct and adrenaline. But after what Asher said, do I even want to hide? Yes and no. I want to prove I can hide well, even if this game seems childish. However, this version of the game seems anything but youthful. I want them to own my body. To take what I'm willing to give. And I want them to give me what they're offering: pleasure I've never experienced before.

"Twenty-two, twenty-three, twenty-four—" Rio continues.

Shit. I need a hiding spot.

Sweat begins to form on my brow as I keep running.

Feeling like I've gone far enough, I stop and look around. There's a wooden crate filled with . . . binoculars.

What the hell? Who needs a whole crate of binoculars?

"I hope you at least make this a little difficult for us!" Zane shouts.

Fuck. Okay. Time for instinct.

Immediately, I'm drawn to the metal shelf. Here goes nothing. The top is easily above their heads, and I can hide behind the cardboard boxes sitting up here.

I feel like I can hear my own heartbeat as I place my foot on the first shelf and give it my weight. There's no creaking sound, so I continue.

"Forty-six, forty-seven, forty-eight—"

I reach the top and give the last shelf my weight. But as I do so, I accidentally nudge a box with my shoe on the shelf below, and it's not silent. Not at all.

"Don't give us too many hints!" Asher taunts.

Fuck. Now I need to hurry. I doubt they'll notice one box moved over slightly—this place isn't exactly squeaky clean. I hurry and make my body as small as possible by bringing my knees to my chest and sitting down behind the boxes. There's a gap so I can see between the two boxes.

"Sixty! Are you ready for us, Spencer?" Rio asks in a singsong voice, still taunting me.

I attempt to slow my breathing, thinking that's going to be the thing that gives me away, and watch for them from my makeshift peephole.

Or peep crack?

I don't see them walk by once, and I strain to hear the smallest sound, but there's nothing. Minutes go by and still nothing. They didn't give up, did they? No. They wouldn't do that. They want their prize as much as I do.

Maybe I still am that good. But before I can mentally pat myself on the back, the two boxes that make up my temporary haven are yanked apart, and my heart is instantly lodged in my throat.

"*Hermanos*! Look what I found over here!" Rio announces to Asher and Zane as he yanks me to the edge of the shelf and hops down, looking up at me.

My breathing picks up in anticipation, waiting to see what he's going to do next—what they're all going to do.

"Well, well. Looks like we caught ourselves a little angel," Zane says as he rounds the corner of another shelf opposite the one I'm on. His eyes are wild and completely zeroed in on me. Asher is right behind him.

"Did you think we wouldn't find you? Or did you make it easy on purpose?" Asher teases. Each step he and Zane take toward me has purpose and, dare I say, swagger.

I thought I could possibly be the one to outsmart them in this scenario, but now I know that I was always the prey.

All three men line themselves up in front of me—eyes and attention on me and my body. It's a heady feeling, having the complete focus of three very powerful and dominant men. Instead of cowering under their gaze, I decide to revel in it. Bask in the heat and fire their passion gives me.

I cross my ankles and lean back slightly to rest my weight on my hands. I'm trying to come off cool when I'm still a panting, needy mess inside. "Well, you caught me. Took you long enough. Now what? Was that all talk, Asher?" My voice comes out a bit breathy, but the challenge is still there.

"Don't poke the devil, Baby. You have three right in front of you, and they all like to play."

Feeling confident I lean forward and give a final push. "Prove it, big guy."

He grabs me around my calves and quite literally yanks me off the shelf but catches me with an arm under my ass and another around my back so we're chest to chest, my legs around his middle. I hook my ankles together to glue myself to him.

"You know exactly how big I am. But now I'll let you feel it in a whole new way."

His promise makes my panties flood, and my need reaches a new level. I grind my pussy along his abs in an attempt to get some friction where I need it.

He denies me relief by flipping me around and setting me on my feet right in front of Rio.

"My turn," Rio growls, then grabs me roughly and brings his mouth to mine. He wastes no time, taking everything I'm offering to him.

He drags me close, as if he's trying to cement our bodies together so we never have to part. He won't have to work too hard; I don't want to leave them either.

His hands slap and grip my ass, then move up to my back and find their way beneath my shirt.

Pulling away from my mouth slightly, he demands, *"Quitarte la blusa ahora." Take off your shirt, now.*

I cross my arms and reach down, grabbing the hem of my plain black shirt. Then, I slowly drag my hands up while keeping eye contact with Rio.

"Serás mi muerte," he pants at the sight of the first sliver of skin revealed on my stomach. *You'll be the death of me.*

Zane seems to have an issue with my teasing because he

steps up behind me, plastering his front to my back so I'm sandwiched between him and Rio, and removes my shirt for me.

"If you'd have gone any slower, I might have died with Rio. And you'd miss our cocks too much," he says in my ear as his breath kisses my skin.

He brings his hands around to my front and begins to undo my jeans. My pussy is weeping for them.

"Now, who's the one going to slow?" I tease and rub my ass against his already hard cock.

"Hear that, Rio? Our girl doesn't want slow."

"Then don't give her slow," Asher grunts out.

His command springs Zane and Rio into action. Rio rids me of my jeans and shoes while Zane unhooks my bra. Zane's hands immediately cup my breasts, and his fingers roll my nipples. I arch into his hands, searching for more. More pleasure. More touch. More everything.

I see Rio and Zane make eye contact, and Zane gives him a nod. Proving they can read each other's minds, Zane lifts my breasts in offering to Rio as Rio brings his mouth to my right breast and bites. But as he bites, his hand snakes in between our bodies and goes right for my clit. I scream out in pain and pleasure. His bite and touch bring both—I yearn for both. He continues to rub my clit and tease my breasts with his mouth, and I grind into his hand.

Rio is a multitasker and deserves an award for it. I feel his hand leave my wanting pussy, then reach past me for Zane. As Rio alternates biting my breasts, sucking my nipples, flicking them with his skilled tongue, and then biting again, he undoes Zane's pants and reaches in. I feel his hand move behind me, up and down Zane's cock, and Zane thrusts into Rio's hand.

"Feel how wet our girl is? Feel her cum on my hand? I barely touched her greedy cunt, and my hand is soaked," Rio breathes to Zane, then goes back to teasing my breasts.

Zane moans and says, "Fuck yes. So goddamn wet for us."

Wanting to give more to Rio, I reach for his cock as well, but he pushes my hand away. He pulls off my nipple with a pop and says to me, "I'm already harder than steel, mi amor. If you get your perfect hands around my dick, I won't last for the plans we have for you."

I grind my pussy against his jeans so I can feel his cock. I need to feel him. I need to feel them all. I need it now.

"Then show me. I need to feel your cocks inside me," I say on a whimper.

At my plea, Zane and Rio rapidly strip off their clothes and I admire their bodies—Rio's tattoo-covered tan skin and Zane's ivory-smooth skin. They both have sculpted abs that don't seem real, and that V that makes all women lose their minds, and their panties.

I turn to Zane and trail my finger down his happy trail and lower to my knees.

"You're supposed to fuck my throat, right? You still want that?" I look up at him as I wrap my hand around his cock and begin to stroke.

"Always, Angel. Always."

I don't ease him into it. I dive right in, taking him as far back in my throat as possible. His hand immediately goes to the back of my head and pushes me back down when I pull away.

Then a set of hands push my knees apart, and a mouth is on my pussy, sucking, licking, teasing. I moan around Zane's dick, causing him to pulse.

"Best pussy I'll ever eat," Rio says below me. "I need this pussy on my tongue morning and night." Then he licks me from my clit to my ass and I'm instantly reminded where Asher intends to be.

"Hurry up and make her come, Rio. I'm dying to get my cock in her sweet ass," I hear Asher demand.

"Happily," Rio responds, sounding like he's drunk. Can a man get drunk on cum? Definitely not. And then he really goes to town, working two fingers then a third into my pussy and attacking that spot inside that will inevitably send me over the edge.

I continue to moan and work my mouth around Zane's length, all of us caught up in the pleasure and heat between us.

"I'm gonna come, Angel. And you're swallowing every drop." Then Zane pulls my hair so hard it stings and really fucks my throat like I was promised. I gag around him and enjoy every second of bringing this man pleasure. When he comes it's with a loud moan and my name on his lips, and like he told me to, I swallow every drop.

Then he drops to his knees next to me and says against my lips, "Such a good fucking girl swallowing for me. Now, come on Rio's face. You know he loves it when you do."

And that's all it takes. I cry out as my pussy spasms and squeezes Rio's fingers which makes him moan against my clit, prolonging my release.

When I come down from the high, I collapse onto Rio's chest and kiss and nibble at his neck. I turn to look at Zane and see he's got his hand around Rio's cock and is working his length by my ass.

"Shit, Z. Shit. I can't come yet," Rio pleads.

Then two sets of hands grab my sides and lower me onto Rio's hard cock. He wasn't kidding—he's ready to go. My pussy stretches and burns slightly as he works himself inside me, and I light up with the slight pain.

I'm exhausted but still alert, anticipating Asher's dick.

"Yes, yes, yes. Don't stop. Please don't stop," I beg.

Once Rio is to the hilt, I feel a hand on my upper back, pushing me forward.

"This devil is ready to play, baby girl. Are you ready?"

"Oh shit." Fear instantly takes over. "Ash, I've never . . . I mean . . ."

"I know," he interrupts. "Trust me. I'll take care of your virgin ass."

It's a simple reassurance, but it's all I need. I do trust him, and I really do want this.

He's already naked and hard, and I feel his cock slide up and down my ass. I hear him spit, and something cold and wet lands on my asshole.

"Breathe, Baby, and relax for me."

Then, he nudges the tip inside. It burns and my eyes water. Rio reaches for my face with both hands and kisses me, lovingly—passionately. Then I feel a hand wedge between mine and Rio's bodies and my body releases the tension I was holding. Asher works his way in more and I cry out.

"Shhh. We're here. Look at you taking two dicks like a good girl—our good girl. I'm going to move now, Spencer. Hold on."

And then Asher fucks my ass. He doesn't hold back either. He doesn't treat me like I'm broken. He treats me like I'm strong.

At first, it doesn't feel all that great, but then that sensation, that desire to fly over the edge, starts to build in my stomach. I turn my head to the side and look to Zane. No words are needed—he knows what I want. He leans in and kisses me through Asher's rough, hot fucking. Rio latches on to my neck, no doubt leaving more marks.

We all moan together as Asher keeps up with his brutal pace.

In and out. In and out.

The slide of his dick in my ass is making obscene sounds—sounds I would normally blush at. But right now, they make me beg.

"Yes, Ash. Yes! Please. It feels so good. But it's too much."

"I need you to feel it all, Baby Girl. Feel how much I want you and will never stop wanting you. Your ass. Your cunt. Your mouth. They were made for us. Made to take our cum. Now take it, Baby. Take every drop."

And when that sensation building inside me bursts, I scream. I scream for mercy. I scream for a god I don't believe in. I scream for my men.

Rio and Asher come with me. Their cocks pulsing and twitching inside me. When we all come back to earth, we collapse into one sweaty, sticky pile, and I pass out.

CHAPTER 15

ASHER

The ding of the elevator causes me to look up and into the bullpen of the fifth floor of the FBI building. There are a lot of people here, considering it's the weekend.

Kowalski looks up from the file in his hands and nonchalantly closes it, placing it under his keyboard. "Hey, Dawson! I wasn't expecting you to come in today. Are you ready to debrief?"

My eyes catch the word "Euphoria" on the front of the file as I take a seat at my desk across from his. "Sure. Berkowitz coming in today?"

Kowalski leans back and sets his feet on his desk, ankles crossed. "He's downstairs getting coffee. Want me to call him and ask to get you a cup?"

"I'm good, thanks," I voice, shaking my head. "What have I missed?"

His eyes dart around the room. "Not much. The APB is still out on Anthony Cole, but it's like the guy is a ghost. His home in Texas has been empty for a while—PD found sheets covering all the furniture like he's a damn royal or something. The last record we have of him is when he flew as a passenger on a private plane to Teterboro."

The elevator dings again, and Berkowitz saunters in with two coffees. "Dawson! You're here."

"I was getting bored sitting around the house." It's not exactly true, but it's not false either. I wouldn't mind being at Spencer's, where I can make her moan my name all day long.

"Dawson is here to give his statement," Kowalski informs.

Berkowitz shifts his weight from foot to foot and pulls his chair away from his desk to sit next to Kowalski. "Awesome. Well, we can take care of that for you." He and Kowalski both pull out their notepads and prepare to write down what I say.

"Tell us what happened first," Kowalski instructs.

Sitting back, I recount details of that night. "I was circulating the room when I saw Ms. Gray slip into the studio next door. I followed her to get her to come back to the event."

Berkowitz scoffs. "You just let her walk away when you knew that psycho was after her? Why didn't you stay by her side? Security one-oh-one."

My eyes narrow. "You're one to talk about security."

He leans forward and grits his teeth. "What's that supposed to mean?"

I stay relaxed in my chair, ignoring his question and continue. "Before we could return, Anthony Cole showed up with five men and quickly surrounded us. I stepped in front of Ms. Gray to shield her from Cole. That pissed him off, and he shot me." I gesture to my shoulder—still in the damn sling. "Then Cole's men carried Ms. Gray and me into a van in the back alley and drove away.

Kowalski is studiously taking notes while Berkowitz eyes me with a furrowed brow and tight jawline.

"What happened next?" Kowalski questions, oblivious to the tension in the room.

"We were taken to a warehouse up north where we were beaten and tortured for information." I aim my next words at Berkowitz. "While Cole was beating me senseless, he let slip that he thought Ms. Gray had stolen something from him when she ran away a few years ago."

Kowalski looks up from his notepad. "Were you able to find out what it was?"

"A list."

Berkowitz pales.

Kowalski squints as his brows drop low. "A list of what?"

Leering at Berkowitz, I answer. "Clients."

"What kind of clients?"

"Turns out Cole has his hands in human trafficking. He's dealt with people all over the country. Some of which are right *here*."

Berkowitz flinches and searches for an exit.

Kowalski finally takes note of the shift in the air. "What's going on? Isaac?"

"Yeah, Isaac." I fish my phone out of my pocket, showing them the evidence on my screen. "Ten thousand dollars, six thousand, eight thousand—care to explain these transactions?"

Kowalski scrutinizes the information on my phone. "What is this?"

The shock on Isaac's face dies. "Nothing. Don't pay any attention to it, Adam." Isaac shoves the phone back in my direction.

Rio always refers to them by their last names so much that I find myself doing the same, rather than Isaac Berkowitz and Adam Kowalski. But it's better than Zane, who I know has more colorful names when he gets irritated with them.

He balls his hands into fists, crushing his pen and notepad, and jumps to his feet. I do the same.

He gets in my face and yells, "You hacked into my bank records?"

"I didn't have to hack anything because I had a warrant. When I called up Marelli and gave him the list, he was all too quick to get a judge's signature on a warrant," I sneer.

The elevator bell dings, and out steps two agents from Internal Affairs, along with Marelli. Isaac spots them, and a whole new level of rage enters his body.

"Isaac, let's talk this out. I'm sure there's an explanation for all of it, right?" Adam reasons, but Isaac ignores him.

"You called IA? You asshole!" He shoves me backward, but I only move one foot back to brace myself. I bring my fist around and land the punch right in his face. His lip splits, and blood gathers in his mouth. He's stopped from swinging back when the IA agents rush over and handcuff his wrists behind his back. Marelli looms behind them.

The outrage on his face satisfies my need to see the moment he realizes his future is over. I recite the lines I've had memorized since my first day in law enforcement. "Issac Berkowitz, you are under arrest for exploitation and coercion. You have the right to remain silent. Anything you say can and will—"

The blood in his teeth becomes visible as he shouts, "I know my damn rights!"

Stepping forward, I bring us toe to toe. The scowl on my face has made greater men quiver and Issac attempts to keep his composure, but I catch a glimpse of trepidation. "Unfortunately, that knowledge will do little for you in prison. Let's see how well you do with three meals a day behind concrete walls and a six-by-six cell where no one will give a shit if you're forced to become someone's bitch, and no one will care if you live or die."

The veins in his neck pulse to a seething rhythm. "You're going to regret this. Anthony will—"

"He doesn't give a fuck what happens to you." The smile on my face is menacing as I pat his cheek. "Enjoy getting raped. It's the least you deserve."

The blood drains from his face. We both know what happens to cops in prison, even when they're placed in protective custody.

I narrow my eyes. "One more thing. Why did you call Sherry the other day when Spencer Gray was here? What was the point? Don't bother denying it; I had your phone records pulled."

He knows he's been caught red-handed. There's no getting out of this with all the evidence I've found.

"I needed to let Cole know where she was without contacting him directly. Sherry Jenkins is always hassling law enforcement on every level for story leads. You and I both know the rumors—a BJ for a tip."

My face turns red. "So, it was just for Cole? Or did you cash in on that little transaction with Sherry?"

He gives me a subtle roll of his eyes. "What do you think?"

"You, son of bitch!" I lunge forward but am held back by a set of arms. I continue to charge forward as an agent backs Berkowitz away. More agents join in my restraint as multiple arms and hands grasp my body but avoid my injury.

"Take him away," Marelli instructs. The two IA agents haul Issac into the elevator as he throws his weight around in an attempt to get free. I shake my head at his feeble efforts.

I don't know where the fuck he thinks he could go. We're in the damn FBI building.

The shock on Adam Kowalski's face seems to be permanent.

Aaron Marelli places a hand on his shoulder. "I hate to do this now, Adam, but we have to ask. Did you know?"

Kowalski rears his head back and finally stands from his chair. "What? No. No, of course not."

Marelli nods his head, satisfied with Adam's answer, and walks into his office.

Adam faces me. "So, what's next?"

My gaze wanders to the window, looking out at the city—the people I swore an oath to protect.

"Now, we watch Anthony Cole's world burn."

CHAPTER 16

RIO

Standing at the window, I wait for the truck—it's been forever since I placed my order. I should be patient, but Asher, Zane, and I are getting fucking tired of sleeping on the floor.

"What are you doing? You're making me nervous," Spencer inquires from her spot amongst the heap of blankets. She's lying on her stomach, watching a show on the new TV Zane bought and installed in her bedroom. She's wearing one of my shirts again and a pair of biker shorts.

"*Nada. No te preocupes.*" I wave a hand at her. *Nothing. Don't worry about it.*

Spencer sits up. "Ever since Zane and Asher left for work, you've been peering out the window. Should we leave? Should I call Hayes and Dahlia and tell them to hurry back from picking up food?"

"It's nothing, Mama. Relax. Watch your show."

As Spencer stands and makes her way to me, the delivery truck pulls up to the curb.

"What's that?"

I smile at her but don't answer. Thirty minutes later, the deliverymen and I have the new bed hauled up the stairs and into Spencer's room.

Spencer stays to the side of the room and throws her arms out wide as I finish putting the sheets, comforter, and pillows in place. "What the hell is this?"

I raise my brows. "It's a bed."

"No, shit, Sherlock." Her frown is full of sarcasm. "I mean, where did you get it, and how the hell are we supposed to live like this when the bed takes up the whole damn room?"

Unable to hold back, I chuckle and comment, "That's what she said."

Spencer rolls her eyes. "Oh my God. You're such a child."

Sitting back against the pillows with my legs crossed and hands behind my head, I rib her further. "Clearly, it fits." I gesture to the open carpet surrounding the bed.

"Barely!" Spencer retorts.

Eyeing the couple of feet from the edge of the bed to where Spencer stands, I tilt my head back and forth. It's not much, but it'll do for now. "Meh. It'll be fine."

"What—I—How—" She stumbles over her words as her brain fights over which question to ask first.

"We'll pick out a frame later." I shrug.

Her mouth continues to open and close in confusion.

Standing from the bed, I saunter up to her and place my hands on her hips. Her shoulders relax at my touch, and masculine, smug satisfaction settles in my chest. "I'm not twenty anymore, Mama. Neither is Zane and Asher. We can't keep sleeping on the floor, and you've had better sleep with all of us in bed with you. And there's no way all of us could fit in your queen-size bed. It was a tight fit with just three of us. So, I came up with a solution."

Spencer peers up at me in disbelief and opens and closes her mouth as she searches for a rebuttal.

I don't give her a chance to speak; I lean down and slam my lips on hers. It takes her a moment to understand what's happening. But once she realizes, she kisses me back with fervor. Our lips push and pull in a blissful dance as our hands skate over each other's bodies.

Mierda. The desire this woman stirs in me is unreal.

I move my hands over her waist and up her torso, cupping her free breasts. Just like any man, I love seeing her boobs in a bra, all pushed up and in my face. But no bra means I get to feel every inch of her mounds, uninhibited.

She lifts my shirt and skims her fingertips over my abs. When she moans, I open my mouth and bite down on her lip, drawing a small drop of blood. She wiggles in an attempt to get closer, and the motion rubs her pussy against my hard cock.

"We got Chinese!" Hayes shouts as the front door opens.

My hands release her tits, and I wrap my arms around her in an embrace. She blows out a breath of frustration and calls out, "Sounds good! We'll be right there!"

"Don't forget to come out clothed!" Dahlia yells back with a snicker.

Spencer's cheeks turn red. "Oh my God." She giggles as she buries her face in my chest.

"No need to be embarrassed, Mama. This is all very natural."

She shakes her head. "It's bad enough that I know they heard me with Asher the other night."

I place my hand under her chin and guide her gaze to mine. "If I thought you'd be into it, I'd make you scream my name over and over while Hayes and Dahlia eat lunch on the other side of the door."

Spencer bites her lip, testing my control, but when her

stomach grumbles, I set aside all plans of tasting her delectable pussy.

I grab her hand and lead her to the door. Tossing back a wink, I tease, "Let's get you fed. I know what happens when you get hangry."

She frowns. "You've never seen me hangry."

We eat and spend the rest of the day wrapped up in each other's arms, while Dahlia and Hayes keep to themselves.

When Asher and Zane get back from work long after the sun has disappeared below the horizon, they find me and Spencer lying on the new bed, watching a true crime documentary about the serial killer, John the Baptist. It blows my mind that this kind of thing is what relaxes my sweet, innocent Spencer.

Spencer perks up when they walk into the room. "Y'all are back!"

A smile spreads over Asher's face, and he sheds his sling and tie, before flinging off his nice shoes. He lies next to her, wrapping his arms around her and kissing her forehead. "Yeah, Princess. We're back."

Spencer settles into the strength of his arms with a content upturn of her lips. She leans into his large frame and soaks up the security he gives her.

Zane strips down and changes into a pair of gray sweatpants that hang low on his hips. He climbs over me to get to Spencer, elbowing me out of the way. She sits up and opens her arms to him. They exchange a brief kiss and lie back down in a restful position.

"How was your day, Angel? What did you and Rio do?"

She releases a tranquil sigh. "Nothing. I should hate it— part of me wants to go running in the morning still, and keep to my routine. But relaxing all day has its appeal as well."

I direct my question to Asher. "How did it go?"

Spencer doesn't miss my purposeful lack of clarity. "How did what go?"

Asher sighs and leans back into the pillows. "Berkowitz tried to deny it until I showed him the evidence. IA has him now. I'm sure the Director and the DA will want to rush the trial."

Spencer leans into Asher's space. "What happened with Berkowitz?"

"His name was on Anthony's list," Zane answers.

Spencer's expression turns implacable. There's no warning before her hand whips out and smacks us each on the arm.

"Hey!" Asher shouts.

"*¡Eso dolió!*" *That hurt.*

"What was that for?" Zane complains.

¡Mierda! Mama knows how to make a playful swat sting.

"That's for keeping *another* thing from me. You should have told me Isaac Berkowitz was on the list. And you should have told me you were confronting him today. You shouldn't have done it alone! If we're in this together, if we want this"—she gestures to all four of us—"to work, then honesty is key. I thought that was established the other night, but it seems y'all needed a reminder." She crosses her arms with a dignified grunt.

Asher gives her a mock glare. "That's the only time you'll get away with something like that."

"I'm not interested in a repeat performance," Zane adds.

"You can hit me anytime, Mama. Just don't get mad when I fuck you raw against the wall." I give her a wink.

"You're impossible, Rio Flores." She tries and fails to suppress a smile.

When we all get a flash of her perfect teeth, we attack. Asher holds her wrists, Zane tickles her stomach, and I go for her feet.

"Oh my God! Stop! Not fair!"

Her laughter rings in the air, filling the room with light.

"I'm going to pee on you!" Spencer threatens.

We all pull our hands away, panting.

"Wouldn't be the first time you peed in front of me," Asher remarks with a smirk.

"That wasn't by choice!" Spencer retorts as a blush spreads across her cheeks and down the length of her soft neck. "Now, tell me what y'all were talking about with Berkowitz."

"His name was on the list," Zane repeats.

Spencer rolls her eyes. "Yes, yes, you said that already. I mean, what happened today?"

Asher fills her in. "I turned him in. He was arrested."

"Oh . . . So you don't . . . Umm . . ."

I snort. "No, Mama. We don't kill everyone who breaks the law." She nods her head. "Only some," I add.

She scrunches her brows. "Okay, that makes sense." Once she's done puzzling out how we operate, she continues. "All right. Now what?"

Asher gathers Spencer in his arms. "Now we enjoy our evening together."

"But what about tomorrow?"

Zane dips his head and kisses her neck tenderly. "We'll deal with that together as well. And the next day and the next."

"So, what're we watching? Is that a documentary?" Asher makes himself more comfortable and places himself and Spencer under the blanket.

Spencer hums her confirmation. "Yes. It's about John the Baptist."

Asher and Zane groan, and I scoff at their contempt.

"What? I think this kind of thing is interesting." Spencer defends her choice.

"Why would we watch a documentary about something we lived through?" Zane argues.

Spencer's eyes light up. "Did you help catch him?"

The rest of the night we spend in bed, finishing the documentary, with Asher and Zane injecting their own comments into the mix. They give Spencer details that the documentary skimmed over or didn't mention at all. Spencer is like a little girl on Christmas morning who got the pony she'd been hoping for. Asher and Zane eat our leftover Chinese takeout from lunch, and Spencer falls asleep as soon as the documentary ends. We quietly tuck ourselves in around her.

Spencer has become our center of gravity. We've always been drawn by this inexplicable need to be in her orbit, to exist where she exists.

She couldn't get rid of us if she tried.

CHAPTER 17

SPENCER

We sit in the surveillance van just a couple of houses down from the address in Poughkeepsie Dahlia gave us. She said she has been to this house many times to visit August, and I have a sneaking suspicion that she lived here for a while herself.

The two-story house is an old Victorian with dirt-covered wood siding and red trim. The driveway is made of gravel, and the porch looks like it needed restructuring about fifty years ago. The dark curtains that hang in all the windows remain closed. The sun recently set, allowing the inky black of night to coat the air.

It's a little cramped with six people in here.

Fifteen passengers, my ass.

There are screens, keyboards, and chairs all in the back—I feel like I walked into an episode of CSI or something. Asher and Rio are in the front seats, while Zane, Dahlia, Hayes, and I are in the back. Zane types away on a keyboard and monitors multiple screens at once.

"What is this? Like a mobile bat cave?" I spin in a circle in my chair, distracting myself from the anticipation of what we're here to do.

Rio snorts. "Bat cave? Like superheroes? We're not superheroes, Mama."

I narrow my eyes. "Agree to disagree on that one." With another glance around, I finally ask the question on my mind. "Not to sound rude, but . . ."

"But what, Angel?"

Scrunching my eyebrows, I finish my thought. "Where the hell did you get all of this stuff?"

This time, Rio, Zane, and Asher laugh together. Dahlia and Hayes look just as confused as I feel.

My head tilts to the side. "What's so funny? Is there some joke I'm not allowed to know? Did you steal it or something?"

Zane answers my question. "No, we didn't steal anything. We purchased everything you see here."

Skeptically, I eye all three of them. "Why do I sense there's more to it?"

Rio leans his head from side to side as he thinks through his vague answer. "When we . . . find those who the justice system has failed to . . . serve justice to, we uhh . . . help ourselves to some of their money."

"Huh?"

"We take money from those we kill." Asher's response is blunt and honest.

I shouldn't be surprised, but I am.

I stare down at my feet. "I'm not sure how I should feel about that."

Rio turns in his seat. "Ultimately, it's your choice how you want to feel about it. But if you're curious, we don't use the money for ourselves. We use it for things like this van."

"Why doesn't that shock me?" Dahlia questions rhetorically.

Of course, they do. Of course, they do shit like this that makes me fall harder for them.

Maybe we could have some fun . . .

Fuck no. Horny Spencer should be satiated by now!

"I got something." Zane interrupts my dirty fantasies.

"What's up?" Asher asks.

"Someone is pulling up the driveway." Zane squints at his screen.

Fuck. What if it's Anthony?

Leaning forward to get a closer look at Zane's monitor, every muscle in my body stiffens as I wait to see who exits the car. I don't have to wait long before I see it's just another damn lackey, and he's carrying . . . groceries?

Dahlia scoots closer to the screen next to me. "That's Greg, fucking asshole."

Last week, Dahlia sat with my guys and gave them all the details she knew about Anthony's "business," including the addresses of prep houses. The locations Anthony uses for parties always change, but she knows about, what I assume is, most of them. Dahlia said this is the house where they keep some of the girls and women "in training," and the children of their victims.

She told them how multiple women have gotten pregnant. Anthony always makes them carry the baby to term and then keeps the child away from the mother so she'll stay in line. The whole practice makes me sick. I cannot imagine going through that, especially at such a young age like Dahlia—she was only sixteen.

"Greg is usually the one to run errands," Dahlia adds.

"Errands? Like he picks up the dry cleaning?" Hayes raises a brow.

Dahlia doesn't react to the joke. "Things like picking up

drugs, transporting girls, and occasionally grocery shopping—everyone has to eat."

I scrunch my brows. "Being high while watching kidnapped victims doesn't sound like a smart business decision."

The tired look in Dahlia's eyes weighs on me. "The drugs aren't for the men, they're for the girls. If the girls become addicted, they're easier to control, and Anthony has the assurance that the girls won't run away—they'll always come back to him for more. He said it's like training dogs to know where their food comes from." She says the last sentence with a sneer on her face.

Zane, Rio, and Asher don't look surprised by the info dump—they know the drill. They're familiar with the dark side of humanity. Hayes's lips grow thin as emotion overtakes him while he looks longingly at Dahlia.

I want to ask, but I'm not entitled to her story. She doesn't need to tell me the details of her tortured past to earn my compassion. She's been a true friend and a silent supporter. She never pried, and I will give her the same in return.

My hand reaches for hers, and I give it a firm squeeze. She turns to me with a shaky smile.

Hayes gives his attention to Zane. "Are you going to let us in on the plan now?"

Asher answers. "Spencer, you're with me. Dahlia, you're with Rio. And Hayes, you're with Zane. Dahlia and Rio will enter through an upstairs window of the room where August is being held. Zane and Hayes will go through the front door, and Spencer and I will go through the back door. Any questions?"

Hayes raises his hand. "Yeah, only about a hundred."

"Save them for later, *hombre*." Rio nods to the house as we see Greg take in the last of the groceries. "It's go time."

CHAPTER 18

RIO

The light *tap tap tap* of footsteps trails behind me as I lead us across the street to the prep house, but Dahlia's steps are inaudible. Before exiting the "mobile bat cave," as Spencer calls it, we all loaded up with the supplies and weapons we would need.

Glancing back at Spencer, I realize we may have given her too much, but she didn't complain. She knows we worry and need the peace of mind that comes with knowing she has everything she may need.

When we near the house, we break into three groups to take our positions. Zane and Hayes camp out under the window on the front porch, and Asher and Spencer lie in wait by the back door while Dahlia and I look for a way into the second-story window. She said that the last time she was here— a few months ago—this was the room where August was held.

I may be a sick fuck myself, but separating a young mother from her child is a type of sadism I refuse to subscribe to.

Dahlia sticks to me like glue as I make my way to an old, battered shed behind the house. There, we find a wooden ladder that has seen better days. She gives me a doubtful look, and I shrug my shoulders in return. We work together to lean the ladder against the house.

We don't have much of a choice when our goal is to get August in and out without having to fire a gun. The more we can keep him out of the crossfire, the better.

"I'll stand and hold the bottom while you climb up. Can you get the window open?" I whisper to her.

She replies with a simple nod, then soundlessly begins her ascent up the rungs. She's so quick and efficient that the weathered wood barely has time to creak. Before I can blink, she has a knife in hand and jimmies the window open. The slide of the pane is smooth, and she climbs over the lip of the window before she waves me up. My journey up the ladder is not as quiet as Dahlia's.

How the hell did she do it?

I pause after each squeak, waiting for the *pendejos* inside to hear us. When they don't come out guns blazing, I prove myself right that they are, in fact, *pendejos*.

I'm surprised this dilapidated thing hasn't completely shattered under my weight. I'm not as big as Asher, but I'm no twig.

As I reach the top, I silently haul myself inside the open window. The room is bare and dusty, and there are three sleeping bags side by side along the far side of the room. The wood floors need refinishing, and the dirty floral wallpaper is bubbling and peeling away from the walls. A standing lamp flickers in the corner of the room.

I stop in my tracks when I'm met with three new faces, rather than one.

Are they running some kind of fucked up boarding school here or something?

One is a little girl who looks like she should be starting

kindergarten. She has a light smattering of freckles across her cheekbones, curly, ash-brown hair, and cerulean eyes. Her lower lip wobbles as she looks at me.

A boy not much older than the girl steps in front of her, shielding her from me. He has sleek obsidian hair, ebony eyes, and a small pink scar that runs from his temple to his jawline. It's jagged, as if it didn't heal properly, and his expression is hard, too hard for someone so young.

Dahlia clings to a little boy who looks to be no older than a toddler. I'm betting it's August—they have the same hazel eyes and straight nose. But where Dahlia's hair is chestnut, August's is a dark coffee. His little arms are secured around her neck, and his face is buried in her shoulder.

"It's okay, it's okay. Mama's here. I'm here." Dahlia smooths a hand up and down his back. Tears line her eyes, but she holds them back with a sniffle.

"Don't leave, Mama." His plea is muffled.

She pulls back and runs her fingers through his wavy hair. "I'm not leaving this time, Bug. You're coming with me."

His eyes light up. "I am?"

"Yes, you are." Dahlia nods with a watery smile.

August's brows furrow, and his lips thin. "But what about Noah and Margaret? Are they coming too?"

Dahlia turns to me for an answer.

"Of course they are," I whisper.

Like I would say no and leave these kids here to rot in this hellhole? Never.

Margaret's curls and cherub face pop up from the side of Noah. "We are? It's been so long since I could go outside." She tugs on Noah's arm. "Can we, Noah? Can we?"

Her excitement at the thought of leaving causes my heart to contract. A young girl like this shouldn't be this happy over something so small as going outside. Walking out the door to play in the yard should be part of her daily routine.

Noah's face turns into a sneer. It's not a face that he should have perfected, yet it is. "We don't know him, Maggie."

Dahlia takes Noah's hand in hers. "This is my friend, Rio. He and his friends are here to get you out." She turns her head to me and explains, "Margaret's mom and Noah's mom are both dancers at Euphoria."

A speck of innocence enters Noah's face. "When can I see my mom?"

Once again, Dahlia turns to me.

Mierda.

"We'll look into it," I vow.

Noah deems my answer acceptable and grabs Margaret's hand, readying themselves to leave.

"Gather your things. We're going out the way we came in."

Footsteps creak outside the bedroom door, and we all freeze. A shadow becomes visible under the door.

I lift my index finger to my mouth in a shushing motion. On light feet, I unsheathe two of my knives as I cross the room to the door. Taking up my position, I wait for the man's next move. The click of a lighter and the distinct scent of cigarette smoke make their way through the door.

A smoke break. Really?

Turning the knob, I crack the door just enough so I can see into the hallway. The walls are pretty much the same as the ones in the kids' bedroom—a different hideous wallpaper, but the same horror movie feel. I spot the staircase leading to the first floor off to the left.

The man's back is to me as he zips up his fly and takes another drag of his cigarette. He has a distinct tattoo of a snake on the back of his neck.

Another man from the bedroom next door exits. He, too,

zips up his fly. Behind him, a half-naked woman lies on the floor sobbing. He slams the door shut and approaches Snake Man.

"Give me one of those."

Snake Man hands over a cigarette and his lighter. The second man lights up and sighs after his first inhale.

"She still needs some work. Cain isn't going to give her the green light for a while."

"*If* he gives her the green light. She could end up like some of the others—never falls in line, so she ends up with a bullet between the eyes." Snake Man taps his forehead in imitation of where the bullet hole would be.

The second man stares off with a wistful look. "I have a good feeling about this one, though. She'll be good at deep throating—I'll teach her."

Yeah. They're both dead.

And looks like we have more guests coming with us.

The second man finishes his cigarette quickly. "I'm going back in. This bitch needs to toughen up. You coming? We can teach her how to take two at once."

Hijos de putas. Sons of bitches.

Snake Man shakes his head. "Not yet. I'll be there in a minute. Get her ready for me."

As soon as the second man disappears into the bedroom, I open the door enough so I can slip out. I creep up right behind him, and he has yet to notice my presence. He places the cigarette back in his mouth for another drag.

Before he can pull it back out, I sheathe one of my knives. My arm wraps around him, and the flat of my palm shoves the cigarette in his mouth completely. The smell of burning flesh invades my nose as he chokes, and I bring my arm around his throat and squeeze, effectively cutting off his air.

"Tell the Devil I say hi," I speak into his ear. I release my hold on his neck, grab his hair at the crown of his head, and pull, exposing his neck fully. Taking the knife in my other hand, I slice his skin from ear to ear. Blood sprays on the wall in front of us.

At least the wall looks better than it did before.

Snake Man's hands cover his wound, but I know how deeply I cut him—there's no stopping the blood flow. He begins to slump, and I use my hands to bring him slowly to the ground so as not to make a sound. By the time his head touches the dirty floor, he's gone.

I return to the kids' bedroom and find Dahlia helping Noah out the window. Margaret and August stand to the side, waiting their turn.

"Go slow, and you'll be fine," she reassures Noah.

He simply nods and places his foot on the first rung, slowly giving the ladder his weight. Once he has both feet in place, there's a loud snap, and Noah's eyes go wide. Margaret and August gasp.

"Fuck," Dahlia curses.

She and I dive forward for Noah's hands. We grasp him tightly and heave him up back into the room. Sticking my head out the window, I find the ladder on the ground, broken in key places.

Voices from beneath our feet drift up and through the floor.

"What the hell was that?"

"How am I supposed to know? Go look."

"Like I'm going walk away so you can get a peek at my cards again."

"You three shut the fuck up! You all can go check it out."

A door downstairs scrapes open, and all hell breaks loose. Shots are fired from both sides. The sound used to hurt my ears, but I'm used to it now. Feminine screams reverberate from the other bedrooms.

I turn back to the doorway as the man from earlier exits the room with the half-naked girl. He's shoving his pathetic dick back into his pants. Without a second thought, I pull out my Glock from its holster and fire. The shot gets him right in the neck, and he goes down quickly. Two more men exit from the other bedrooms.

Pop, pop.

I get each with one shot. They fall on top of the other two men.

Glancing over my shoulder, I find Dahlia with all three kids gathered and ready to go. "On me!" I shout over the noise.

She nods her head once and ushers the kids forward, right behind me.

I step out into the hallway and nod to each of the bedrooms. "I'm going to grab the girls in each room. If anyone comes up the stairs, you shoot."

"Got it," Dahlia confirms.

Kicking in the first door, I find the woman from earlier lying in a pool of her own blood. Her eyes are open but lifeless.

Fuck!

I find the same scene in the remaining two bedrooms.

Now I wish I would have taken my time with them. I wish I would have made it hurt more. But this moment isn't for "should have" and "could have;" I have four lives depending on me to get them out of here.

"Stay close!"

I take a few steps down the staircase and peek down to assess the situation. Asher and Spencer are having a shoot-out with two men at the back of the house, in the kitchen, and Zane and Hayes are just outside the front door in a standoff with a few men hiding behind furniture in the living room.

Drawing the fire of the men in the living room, I aim my gun at them and fire off three shots. Two of them pop up from the backside of the couch to shoot at me, but Zane and Hayes get each of them before the men can get a shot off at me. The last man stands from behind an armchair. He raises his hands in retreat, but I don't give a fuck. I empty my Glock into the *pendejo*.

If he wanted mercy, he chose the wrong business to be in.

Zane and Hayes advance forward and around the backside of the kitchen, shooting the remaining two in the back.

"Clear!" Asher announces.

"Clear!" Zane replies.

I shout out the final response. "Clear!"

We finish our descent down the stairs, shielding the dead bodies from the kids' view, and find Asher, Spencer, Hayes, and Zane in the kitchen.

"We need to move n—" Zane chokes on his words as he spies the two bonus children.

"Guys, this is Noah and Margaret." I give my friends big eyes, indicating they need to tread lightly.

Spencer is the first to step up. "Hi, Margaret and Noah. My name is Spencer. What do you say we get out of here and get some ice cream?"

Margaret jumps up and down. "Oh yes! Please, please, please!"

Zane's face turns soft as he kneels in front of Margaret. "Anything you want, Sweetheart."

CHAPTER 19

SPENCER

We're even more cramped than we were before, but none of us mind.

Margaret sits in Zane's lap and talks his ear off. He shows her games on his computers and teaches her how to play Snake and Minesweeper. Noah sits with Hayes but hovers over Margaret. August refuses to leave Dahlia and requests that they sit near his friends.

I wish my brain would focus on the good. I wish I could just be happy that these kids are safe now, but my mind wanders.

What happened to them in that house?

What did Anthony do to them?

How often were they allowed to see their moms?

Rio's hand reaches from the front seat and lands on my knee. "Hey. Don't stew on it, Mama. We got them out of there. They're safe now. That's all that matters."

Fuck these men and their ability to always read my mind.

Glancing up, I notice Asher listening in on our conversation.

"I just can't help but wonder." I fiddle with my hands in my lap.

Rio stops me by interlacing his fingers with mine. "I know. And one day, they may tell us. But for now, a win is a win."

The curiosity of my brain doesn't shut off just yet. "Was there anyone else in the house?"

"There was." His mouth thins in displeasure.

"Where are—"

"They were killed before I could get to them. It seems Anthony's policy is to leave no survivors. People are just a commodity to him, and our planet is busting at the seams with his chosen merchandise. He believes he can afford to kill a few because he knows he can easily replace them."

I trace circles on the back of his hand with my thumb. "You tried—that counts for something. Don't blame yourself."

Rio's jaw tenses visibly. "I'm not. I'm fuming that someone like Anthony still walks around as a free man. He doesn't deserve to breathe fresh air. He doesn't deserve to experience this life while he ruins it for so many others. He's a dead man. Vengeance will come to him soon."

My eyes lock with Asher's in the rearview mirror as he drives the van. The fury stirring there tells me all I need to know.

He plans on putting a bullet in Anthony's skull.

THE REST of the ride is silent. We stopped at St. Barnabas so Elena could check each of the children. She said that Noah's scar will fade over time but will probably always be visible. Noah let slip that one of Anthony's men cut him with a broken beer bottle. He didn't offer more detail than that.

She tested all three kids for every sickness, disease, and infection under the sun. Besides being slightly dehydrated, they're all healthy.

We left Elena in the late morning and decided to take the kids out for ice cream. The stop at the ice cream shop was supposed to be short, but Margaret wanted to try every flavor. Zane wasn't able to say no to her—anyone who can is heartless. The teenager managing the shop was more than happy to indulge Margaret in her every whim.

Now, the kids are snuggled together on the floor of my living room, watching a movie. Their ice cream is smeared all over their mouths, and they each wear a smile on their faces.

Dahlia sits next to August with her arm around his shoulders. Her aura is lighter now that she has August by her side. I never noticed the air of sadness that followed her everywhere before.

Hayes sits on the other side of Dahlia. His gentle, firm foundation gives Dahlia the confidence and security she needs to enjoy this time with her son. He constantly cracks jokes that force innocent giggles from August, Noah, and Margaret.

The guys and I lurk in the kitchen, observing the Hallmark scene taking place in my living room. We should probably give them some space, but I think we're all a little wary of leaving the kids alone so soon.

The kids finish their ice cream and finally drift off to sleep just after lunch. They lean against each other, with Margaret in the middle, and hold each other's hands.

Hayes leaves Dahlia, who is watching August sleep, and tiptoes over to us in the kitchen. "I want to take them home." He holds a hand up as we prepare to argue. "Anthony is going to be looking for you, and he'll come ready to fight. It's not fair to put these kids in the middle when they just got away from all that shit."

Zane raises his brows. "Where would you take them that's safer than here?"

"My home in Boston." Hayes crosses his arms.

My lips twist into a frown. "I thought you lived here in the city."

"I do, but I'm from Boston. My parents live there and pay for very expensive security." Hayes directs his last sentence to the guys.

What the fuck is going on?

Asher, Rio, and Zane exchange looks, participating in a secret conversation that only they understand. They give Hayes a nod, which is all the confirmation he needs.

I really need to purchase that damn book, *"How to Decipher the Grunts and Gestures of Cavemen."* I'm tired of being left out of these exchanges.

Hayes pulls out his phone and gives us his back, but we can still hear his conversation. "Kieran, I need a ride home, and I'm bringing a few guests." He nods his head as the man on the other end of the line speaks, then hangs up without so much as a goodbye.

Ugh. Men.

Hayes stows his phone in his pocket and informs us, "My bodyguard will be here soon. We'll be on the road in a couple of hours."

My head drops to a concerned angle. "You have a—"

"Do you need anything?" Asher interrupts.

"No, we're good. The car will be stocked."

I put my hands out, halting everyone. "Hold on a goddamn minute." I receive four puzzled looks. "Why do you have a bodyguard? And you told me you lived in the city."

Hayes looks like a deer caught in headlights. "Uhh . . ."

Rio places an arm around my waist and guides me towards my bedroom. "I'll explain when you're older."

"The hell?"

"Nap first. Explanations later." Rio forces me to lie down and tucks me in under the blankets.

I heave out an exasperated breath and flop my hands down on either side of me.

Rio smirks. "Okay, you convinced me. I'll catch a few Z's with you." He lifts the corner of the comforter and urges me to scoot over.

"What? That's not what I said."

"No need to deny it. You all but shouted it at me." He rolls me onto my side and aligns his body with mine. "Sleep, Mama. We'll wake up in time to say goodbye."

Sighing, I settle into his arms, but I don't sleep whatsoever.

When Hayes's bodyguard arrives, he pulls up to the curb in a blacked-out SUV. Dahlia showers Hayes with a million questions, all of which he agrees to answer in the car. Margaret gives us a tearful goodbye while Noah tries to remain emotionless. He and August comfort Margaret, coaxing her into the vehicle.

As I hug Dahlia, I whisper in her ear, "Promise me you'll keep me updated, babe."

She pulls back with our arms still around each other. "I promise. And you'll do the same?"

"Of course."

We wipe our tears as she gets in the car, followed by Hayes. Kieran, Hayes's bodyguard, shuts the door behind them and gets into the passenger seat, before the other man in the driver's seat steers the car into traffic.

Strong ivory arms hold me together, gifting me with reassurance and sympathy. "They'll be okay. Everything will be okay."

"How can you be so sure?"

"Trust me, Angel." Zane places a tender kiss on my head.

"I do."

CHAPTER 20

SPENCER

"*¡Cállete, cabrón!* I'm telling you, that piece is supposed to go right here!" *Shut up, bastard.* Rio points to what I think is supposed to be the headboard of my new bedframe. He and I have been lazing about all day.

The guys are still serious about never leaving me alone, especially now.

We picked out the frame online together, but delivery was delayed. So now, all three guys are attempting to assemble it but have been unsuccessful so far. Rio must have chosen the most complicated frame in existence because they have been at this for over an hour.

Zane is in those tempting gray sweatpants and sexy glasses. "The instructions clearly state that it goes here." He's standing by the foot of the bed.

"But it clearly will fit right here," Asher argues. When he got home, he changed into a pair of basketball shorts and a loose tee. His suits are sexy, but seeing him so casual is just as hot.

"How would you know? I'm the one with the instructions," Zane shoots back.

"Anyone with eyes can see it goes here." Asher points to where he's standing by the side.

"You're the one who can't get past level two on Tetris!" Rio accuses Asher.

He has a good point.

Asher's eyes narrow, and he frowns. "What does that have to do with putting a bedframe together?"

Another good point.

"It has everything to do with it!" Rio throws his hands up.

Zane rubs his eyes. "You both sound like a couple of dumbasses. Just read the damn directions so we can get this done and go to bed."

This is like watching a glacier melt.

I've been sitting in the corner this whole time, watching them bicker like grumpy old men. They keep saying they're almost done, but we're still here. Various pieces of dark walnut stained wood, matte black hardware, and several screws in different sizes are strewn about.

"I'm just going to . . ." I get to my feet and point to the open bedroom door.

Zane motions for me to stay. "Sit your pretty little ass back down, Angel. We're almost done."

Crossing my arms, I express my annoyance. "My pretty little ass is going numb over here."

Rio's eyes light up. "Need some help with that, Mama?"

I widen my stance and give him a piercing stare. "Navarro Juan Carlos de la Cruz Flores, if your hands come anywhere near my ass right now, I'll cut them off."

"I'm going to marry that woman," Rio mock-whispers to Asher while his heart eyes remain fixed on me.

On a normal day, I wouldn't be able to help but smile. But it's been three days since Hayes, Dahlia, and the kids left for Boston, and I'm going insane. I haven't left the apartment at all. I was overruled when I suggested opening the studio and gallery back up. I'm not eager to get back to the two places where awful things have happened, but I'm determined to take control of my life again.

Stomping into the kitchen, I yell over my shoulder, "I can't keep doing this. I need out!"

A large, calloused hand stops me. "Talk to us, Princess. What's going on?"

Spinning on my heels, I barely hold back a scream of frustration. "I. Need. Out."

Rio places a hand on the small of my back. "Out of what? This?" His hand waves to the three of them.

Jerking my head back, I reply, indignantly, "What the hell are you talking about?"

Asher places his hands on his hips. "Are you breaking up with us?"

"Seriously? No! I just need out of the apartment. I'm going crazy! I want to go for a run. I want to create in my studio. I can't just stay in here for the rest of my life." My fingertips massage my temples.

Zane envelops my hand in his. "You know why—"

"I know Anthony is still out there. I know I'm still in danger —I get it! But I've been living with that for three years! I'm tired of living my life in fear of him! Every choice, every movement has been about staying hidden. I can't keep doing it."

"It's different now." Zane's hands raise to hold my face, and his thumbs wipe away the tears I didn't know were there.

The waterworks have begun, and I can't turn them off.

"How?" My voice squeaks.

"You have us." Zane pulls me into his arms, and I'm unable to resist the support he's offering.

My face grows even more damp from unbidden tears as I bury my face in his chest. Two more sets of hands work to release the tension from my body by kneading the muscles in my back and running through my wavy hair.

God, these men know how to silence all the worries in my mind. Not fair.

Three. Fucking. Years.

I have lived in fear this whole time. I can't let Anthony continue to control my life. Even though I ran away, he's still been this invisible presence, dictating my every move.

No more.

It's Anthony's turn to hide.

CHAPTER 21

SPENCER

Last night, after my meltdown, my three men became extra attentive. Asher fixed me up a late-night snack while Rio and Zane worked swiftly to finish building the bed frame. We all climbed into bed and fell asleep to some cooking competition show Asher turned on.

Rio attached himself to my back like a koala with Zane on the other side of him. I ended up sleeping half on top of Asher and leaving behind a small drool spot on his chest. Not that he needed another embarrassing moment in his arsenal to use against me. Listening to me pee is horrifying enough to last many lifetimes.

When my alarm goes off in the morning, I reach my hand out to turn it off, but the noise persists.

"Stop smacking me in the face. I'll make it stop," Asher grumbles.

Oops.

A rush of cold air across my bare legs sends a shock to my consciousness.

"What the fuck?" I crack an eye open and am met with a smiling Rio.

"Rise and shine, Sleeping Beauty!"

"Are you crazy? It's six a.m." Rolling over to use Asher's body heat to warm me up, I find his spot vacant. I open my eyes and find Zane and Asher changing into . . . workout clothes?

A naked Asher peeks back at me and winks. "You can stare all you want, Princess. But a picture will last longer."

My mouth drops open. "I wasn't—I mean—What's going on?"

Rio stands and pulls me up with him. "We're going to the gym. Duh."

Squealing, I jump and wrap my legs around his waist. Thankfully, he catches me as both of his hands cup my ass. "Thank you, thank you, thank you!" I pepper his face with kisses.

"If I knew this would be your reaction, I would have made this happen sooner."

Zane appears behind Rio. "Share the love, Angel. Where are my kisses?"

Rio gives my ass one more squeeze before handing me over to Zane. I give him the same treatment while Asher stands off to the side, pretending to ignore the scene in front of him and checking his watch.

"We should probably get going," he suggests.

Zane sets me down on my feet, and I walk right up to him. I fist his shirt at the center of his chest and pull until he leans down. The kiss I plant on his lips is slow and passionate. He follows my lead for the first time and moves his lips with mine.

We break the kiss at the same time and rest our heads together.

"Thank you," I whisper reverently.

His voice is gruff. "You only need to ask, and I'll give you the world, Princess."

As we take off down the street, I relish the movement of my limbs and the way my body warms. Rio keeps pace on my left, and Zane and Asher stick right behind us.

The morning is cool, and the sun is beginning to paint the sky in beautiful shades of pink, yellow, and orange. It's the perfect morning.

Besides the fact that a literal serial killer is after you.

Even though Inner Spencer is right, I refuse to let that dampen the mood.

Out of the corner of my eye, I take a quick look at Rio. He's concentrated on our surroundings, searching for any sign of a threat.

If my life were a cartoon, a light bulb would appear above my head right now. I'm very aware of the seriousness of our circumstances, but we deserve to have fun at the same time.

Lengthening my stride, my speed picks up from a fast jog to a run. Rio notices and increases his pace to match mine. We make eye contact, and I shoot him a crafty smirk.

"*Ni te atrevas,*" he pants in between breaths. *Don't you dare.*

My smile grows, and I break into an all-out sprint. "Catch me if you can."

"*Mierda,*" Rio hisses.

"Ah, shit," Zane complains.

"Fuck," Asher grunts.

The laugh that comes out of me is spirited and free. The smacking of their tennis shoes on the pavement and their heavy breaths mingle with mine. I know I can't outrun them—that isn't the goal.

I know I'm playing with fire here, but I enjoy provoking their feral side. The side that calls to an aspect of myself I didn't realize was suppressed. They're going to be so pissed at me, but I know I'll find pleasure in their punishment.

Zane's shoes appear next to mine as he catches up with me. A glance over my shoulder informs me that Asher and Rio are right on our heels, just as I expected.

I stumble slightly as I elbow Zane in the side, causing him to grunt. He finally gives me a smile and a shake of his head.

When we round the corner and the sign for Joey's Gym comes into view, I push myself one last time.

"You've got to be kidding me," Asher bitches.

Rio laughs, and Zane stays right by my side.

Stopping abruptly at the entrance, I lean against the wall as my labored breaths saw in and out of my lungs. Zane paces next to me with his hands on his head—he's barely out of breath. Asher bends over to stretch his hamstrings, and Rio falls face first on the pavement with arms spread out on either side.

"You really are trying to kill me." The sidewalk muffles Rio's claim.

My chuckle is barely there from being so out of breath. "You wouldn't feel like you were dying if you'd work on your cardio more."

Zane grimaces as he eyes Rio on the ground. "You know that's not sanitary, right?"

Rio lifts his head for a second to respond. "I'm building my immune system."

"If that's what you want to call it." Asher's lip curls in disdain.

Shaking my head at their squabbling, I walk inside with all three of my men following right behind me. My focus immediately goes to the front desk, and I find Joey standing there as usual. When he sees me, his eyes light up for a split second before the glee vanishes and is replaced with his usual rough exterior.

"You look like shit." His words are gruff, but I know what they mean.

My heart warms, and the corners of my mouth curve. "And you look like a shriveled-up dick."

He rounds the desk and beelines right for me. His arms encircle my body, and I freeze in shock. After a moment, I sink into the affection and return the gesture.

"You really scared me the other night." He sounds choked up.

My tears threaten to fall. "Sorry about that," I whisper.

He pulls back and looks me up and down. "How does the other guy look?"

My face hardens as I think of how Anthony is still walking around a free man. He dishes out pain and suffering like he's a fucking sadistic Santa Claus. He takes what he wants because he believes he's untouchable—invincible even.

He doesn't get to feel safe. He doesn't get to live life carefree.

He'll feel my vengeance soon enough. My wrath will no longer be hidden behind veils in the shadows. Anthony is the one who should be plagued with nightmares and fearful of every person he meets.

"He'll be cold and six feet under soon."

CHAPTER 22

SPENCER

Apparently, my recent kidnapping means nothing to Joey because he puts me through hell. Squat jumps, burpees, mountain climbers, planks. By the time I'm done, I'm drenched in sweat and smell like a locker room. I'm sure my face is redder than a damn red flag.

The guys do their own workouts and look like fucking Greek gods when they're done. Their sculpted bodies next to my wet dog look must look like a comical juxtaposition.

Whatever higher power is in charge is having a good laugh.

The run back to my apartment is more relaxed, but I'm still a gross mess of fetid aroma, and my face is still so red that I could be the new campaign for Target.

When we get through the door, I literally stick my head in the freezer, and my action is met with snickers.

I raise my hand in the air with a certain finger pointed in their direction. "Laugh it up. See what it gets you later."

A pair of hands slap my ass, causing me to yelp.

"You can stand like this all day, Mama. I'm enjoying the view."

My panties flood with arousal, and my pussy pulses with need. Rio doesn't give me any room to move when I stand upright. With my hair up, he has easy access to my neck, and he takes full advantage by kissing his way down to my shoulder. I moan when he drags his teeth over the spot where my neck and shoulder meet.

When I'm ready to turn around and ride him right there in the middle of the kitchen, Rio takes a step back, turning to Zane. "I'm going to hop in the shower. Come help me wash?"

Zane gives Rio and me a mischievous smile. "Absolutely."

Rio leads the way to my bedroom with a smug look on his face, and Zane walks with his arm around Rio. He pulls Rio into his side and nips at Rio's neck.

I become flushed watching their interaction and rub my thighs together, but the ache in my core is persistent.

Asher stands behind me, lining his body with mine, and runs his hands down my sides to my hips. "I think that was an invitation, Princess," he whispers seductively in my ear.

"But . . . shouldn't they have some time to themselves?"

"If they wanted to be alone, they wouldn't have announced where they were going," Asher reasons.

The water in my shower turns on, and the image of Zane's and Rio's slick, wet bodies up against each other flashes in my mind.

"I suggest you get your cute little ass in there before they finish without you."

My mouth opens and closes. "Um—I—Uh—"

He smacks my ass with a chuckle and turns to the fridge, gathering ingredients to make himself a sandwich.

On unsteady feet, I tread toward the bathroom. Zane's moans meet my ears as I get closer, and my skin prickles with anticipation.

What if they don't want me here? What if Asher was wrong?

All anxious thoughts leave me at the sight before me, and a desperate need radiates through my body.

Through the glass of the shower door, I can see Rio on his knees in front of Zane, moving his head back and forth. I watch as Zane's hard cock slides in and out of Rio's mouth. Rio hollows his cheeks as he pulls back and uses his tongue to slide along the underside of Zane's length.

My breaths come quickly, and my chest heaves.

I need them. I want them.

Zane's head is thrown back in pleasure, and his hands are on the back of Rio's head, guiding Rio back and forth. He thrusts his hips forward in time with Rio.

My hand glides down the center of my chest and dives into my leggings. I find my pussy soaking wet. My fingers slip right to my clit, moving in circles around it. I have to bite my lip to keep quiet.

"Such a good boy sucking my dick."

Rio moans with Zane's cock in his mouth.

I flick my bundle of nerves over and over while my other hand snakes up under my bra, and I cup my heavy breast. My nipple hardens to a point as I pinch and twist, riding the edge of pain and pleasure.

Zane's eyes open and connect with mine. His pupils are blown wide with lust, and a satisfied look crosses his face. "We have a spectator, Rio. Show my Angel how good you are at making me come."

The corner of Rio's mouth turns up. He brings one of his hands to Zane's ass, and I see his finger disappear into Zane's hole. His hand moves in and out, causing Zane to cry out. His movements become more frantic as he approaches his peak.

Two of my fingers enter my core, but it's not enough. My thumb rubs my clit as I move my fingers in and out.

Zane shouts his release as Rio swallows it down, and a

moan slips free from my mouth as I fall over the edge into bliss. My hand floods with my climax.

When I open my eyes, Rio stands, licking his lips, and Zane keeps eye contact with me as he takes Rio's cock in his hand and begins pumping.

A whimper escapes my lips, and the need in my core builds again.

"Come shower with us, Angel."

Zane's invitation makes my body crave their touch. I swiftly strip out of my clothes and toss them aside.

As I take my first step, Rio speaks up. "Hold on a second." He shoots Zane a wink and turns back to me. "Crawl to us, Mama."

Holy shit. Why is that fucking hot?

Dropping to my hands and knees, I crawl across the cold tile. Zane opens the glass shower door for me and drops of water spray my skin. Shivering, I crawl across the wet tiled flooring

I sit back on my heels as their gazes encompass my naked body. They look at me with desire burning in their eyes.

I've always avoided this kind of attention, but I find myself craving the next moment they look at me like this. They look at me like I'm delicate, sexy, and fierce—words I never thought I'd associate with myself.

Zane is now stroking his own length as well as Rio's, and I bite my lip.

"What's next, Angel?"

Giving them my best seductive expression, I go up on my knees in front of Rio and rest my hands on his thighs. "Help me a little?" I ask Zane.

He raises a brow but catches on when I stick my tongue out and move to lick the bead of precum at the tip of Rio's cock. Zane keeps his hand around Rio's shaft and rubs his tip up and down my waiting tongue. Rio's salty taste makes me desperate for more, and Rio moans.

"You're so beautiful on your knees for us, Spencer," Zane growls.

I lean forward and suck Rio's cock into my mouth.

"Damn, Baby Girl. You're desperate for my dick, aren't you?"

"Oh yes, she is," Zane answers for me.

Moaning, I bob my head back and forth. Then I drag my tongue through his slit. Taking Zane's length in my hand, I pump him in sync with my movements up and down Rio's dick.

"Fuck! That feels good," Zane exclaims.

Smirking, I let go of Rio's length with a pop and replace my mouth with my hand. I shift on my knees and urge Zane closer. He shuffles, and then I give Zane the same treatment.

"Shit, this is hot," Rio groans. "Don't stop, Spencer."

I switch back and forth between the two—sucking one while I stroke the other. Ignoring the ache in my knees, I squeeze my thighs together, longing for my core to be filled.

It's not long before they're both thrusting their hips at erratic paces.

"I'm going to come, Spencer. Pull back if you don't want to swallow," Rio warns.

I feel his dick swell and pull back, moving my fist up and down. He groans as he comes, and I direct his release at my chest. His cum splashes across my bare breasts.

Fucking hell. That's hot.

"*Eres mi reina,*" Rio pants. *You are my queen.*

"Fuck, fuck, fuck!" Zane yells. His dick becomes impossibly hard and his release paints my skin right over Rio's cum.

Curiously, I drag my fingers across my chest and bring them to my mouth, sucking down their cum. I moan and glide my other hand down my stomach, aiming for my pussy. The need to climax is intense.

But before I can touch myself, Zane grabs my wrist. "Don't take our fun away, Angel. Your pleasure is our job." He smirks and lifts me to my feet.

"Z, you haven't let her come yet?" Asher makes a tsking sound and strolls into the bathroom. Steam fills the bathroom, making it hard to see the details of his body.

"We were just getting to that, Ash," Rio shoots back teasingly.

Asher's response sounds mischievous. "Hmm. Maybe you need some guidance."

Fuck. Is he joining us? Oh God. Please, please, please.

I can see him move, and then he opens the shower door. I get an eyeful of his muscular, naked body. His dick is hard as he takes in the mess Rio and Zane have made of me.

"You three sure have been busy," Asher states with a wink. He stands right behind me, grabbing my hips and pulling me back so my ass is against his crotch. His thick length, slick with water, slips in between my cheeks. He moves his hips, making his dick slides up and down, teasing my back hole.

I can feel Zane and Rio's eyes on us, watching every movement and memorizing each of my reactions.

"Shit," I curse lightly, but they still hear it.

"Tell me how that feels, Princess." Asher's hot breath caresses my ear.

"Good," I rely shakily.

His hands slide forward and south, cupping my pussy. "You can do better than that."

"It feels *really* good."

Before I know it, Asher steps back, and a resounding *slap* echoes off the glass of the shower. Finally, a stinging sensation radiates from my ass.

"Did you just—"

"Hell yes, I did. That was for the sass. Now, tell me how this makes you feel." He emphasizes his command by repeating his earlier movements and swiping his fingers through my slit, flicking my clit.

"Shit! I love it. I need it. I need to come. Please, make me come," I answer breathlessly.

"That was better," he growls. "As you wish, Princess." He uses his hand to lift my leg, exposing my pussy to Rio and Zane. "I think it's time you two return the favor."

"*Sí, por favor.*" *Yes, please.*

"I was planning on it," Zane replies smugly.

Zane drags his tongue across my breasts, sucking one nipple and then the other. He tastes his and Rio's cum mixed together. Then he slides to his knees, keeping his mouth against my skin as he sinks down.

Rio approaches me next and does the same. He bites down on one of my stiff peaks while his hand fondles the other, making me cry out as I am quickly brought to that line of pain and pleasure. When he falls to his knees, Asher places my leg on Rio's shoulder.

Asher leans back into the cold tiled wall behind him and keeps his grip on my leg. "Make our girl come," he commands.

Zane and Rio waste no time diving in. Their tongues work in tandem, licking my pussy. One enters my core, moving in and out, while the other rapidly flicks my clit.

I bring my hands up and grasp onto Asher's neck, needing something to hold onto while these men make it impossible to stand.

"Your cunt is so needy, Princess."

His filthy words cause me to whimper.

"I'm going to take this ass again. All day, you've been

flaunting it in my face. Now it's mine. I'm going to fuck your ass good and hard."

The ache in my pussy becomes unbearable. "Fuck. Yes! Do it."

My affirmation is all Asher needs. He pushes his mushroom tip into my ass. The ring of muscle stretches around his thickness, but the pain of the stretch is dulled as Rio and Zane continue driving me crazy by running their tongues up and down my pussy.

"That's it. Relax and let me in," Asher praises.

I remove one hand from his neck and wrap it behind me, grabbing Asher's hip. Urging him forward, Asher's dick enters further. Once he's completely inside me, I breathe through the staggering feeling of being full. Everyone pauses at my deep breaths.

"Fuck me. I need to come," I plead.

None of them hesitate. Asher plunges his dick in and out of my ass while Rio and Zane move their tongues through my cunt faster. A tingling sensation builds and builds low in my belly as I approach the peak, and my legs begin to shake.

Asher brings one of his hands to my breast, tweaking my nipple then soothing away the pain.

"Holy shit!" I cry out as I completely lose control and fall over the edge into a hurricane of ecstasy. My puckered hole tightens around Asher's dick, and his body tenses as he follows me with his own climax.

Zane and Rio don't stop until my muscles relax, and I sag against Asher's firm body. Asher smooths his hands up and down my arms in comfort as Zane and Rio kiss their way up my body.

Tenderly, I'm passed from man to man. They work together, washing my body and hair, kneading my muscles, and stroking my skin. Their fingers massage my scalp as they work in the conditioner.

I keep my eyes closed the entire time, close to falling asleep while standing. Once I'm all clean, the water is turned off, and I'm wrapped in a fluffy towel. One of them lifts and carries me to the bed, and I'm delicately placed under the covers. They all gather around me as we laze in our perfect moment.

"I love you, Angel."

"*Te amo.*" *I love you.*

"I love you, Princess."

"I love you too."

CHAPTER 23

SPENCER

The *thump thump thump* of the large bass beats against my chest, and the stench of sweaty bodies mixes with alcohol and stale smoke. The club lights flash and dance around the floor, adding to the nightlife vibe. It's packed in here, but I shouldn't be surprised—it's a Friday night in New York City.

Sipping my drink, I move side to side on my stool as I pull down the hem of the dress Rio picked out. The bar top is crowded with people waiting to put in their order for drinks.

I was awoken from my sex-induced nap with food and an invitation—that I wasn't allowed to refuse—to a night out at a club with my guys. Although, there was a small argument over the intelligence behind the decision. My suggestion that going out may help bring Anthony and Pierce out of hiding almost shut down the whole plan. But Rio swiftly ended the discussion by saying that they all needed to take their girlfriend on a proper date.

Rio pulled out a dress I didn't know existed from the back of my closet and pushed me to try it on for them. It's a miracle

I was able to do my makeup and hair without Dahlia and Alma's help. And when I came out all dolled up, I think I almost had a repeat performance of our shower escapades. I dashed out the door and was promised that I would pay for teasing them later.

I was dancing with Rio and Zane for a while, but needed a break so Asher helped me to the bar to order a drink.

Asher stands behind my stool as I rest my feet and sip my rosemary vodka tonic. I lean my head back against his chest, and he wraps an arm around me. The music is too loud for a normal conversation, so we speak with light touches and flirty glances.

I'm jostled when a man pushes his way past the waiting line to get to the bartender fixing drinks across from me. Leaning too far to the right, I almost fall off the stool. I brace for the impact, but it never comes. Asher's quick reflexes have him reacting without thought and he rights me on the stool.

"Hey! I want a drink!" The pushy man's whiny voice can barely be heard over the music.

Ew.

The bartender's expression indicates he recognizes the man, and he stops in the middle of making a margarita to quickly whip up a martini with extra olives.

The man has a baby face and gelled blond hair. His clothes scream rich yacht club and "I live off of Daddy's money." He looks like he just turned twenty-one yesterday.

Asher glares at the man as he leans against the bar and takes a big gulp of his drink. I tap Asher's hand and shake my head. Asher reigns in his anger as his jaw tenses, and he places his hands on my shoulders.

The man turns to me. He looks me up and down with calculation in his eyes, completely ignoring Asher's hands on me.

Fucking hell. I'm going to need a shower.

"How much?" he asks with a creepy half-smile.

Asher's grip on my shoulders tightens.

"Excuse me?" I furrow my eyebrows.

"For the night. How much?" He looks me up and down again, his eyes snagging on my cleavage. "With that dress and those legs . . . five thousand."

Is this bitch asking for what I think he's asking for?

Asher's hands begin to quiver.

My jaw drops at this fucker's proposition. He must have had a gallon of audacity with his morning coffee.

The man places his sweaty palm on my knee and leans close. "I may even let you come, too," he adds with a wink.

Is that supposed to sweeten this bullshit deal?

I place my hand on Asher's, reassuring him that I've got this, but I know he's ready to explode.

The man's thumb strokes the inside of my knee.

Giving him a fake smile, I grab his wrist and pull it to an unnatural angle. He drops his martini on the floor and the glass breaks as he shouts in pain.

His other hand rears back to slap my face. I dodge and twist his wrist further, so he has no choice but to fall against the bar. He tries to push up, but I push down with my upper body.

The only action he's going to get tonight is my boobs against his back because I'll fucking castrate this prick.

"What the fuck!"

I bring my mouth to his ear. "Touch me again, and I'll fucking kill you. Slowly." I give him one more shove, then let go and sit back down on my stool. Waving my hand in the air, I ignore the gawking bystanders and shout at the bartender. "We need another drink over here!"

The man is panting as he stands. His chin raises, and his eyes seem to bulge. "No cunt is worth your brand of crazy."

In a flash, the man is on the floor with three scary-looking fuckers surrounding him. A few people gasp and back away. Some don't even notice what's going on.

Those are my men.

Zane places his foot on the man's chest. "You're lucky. She was going to let you walk away with nothing more than a few strained muscles."

Rio crouches down and shakes his head. "But you had to go and touch what isn't yours."

"That makes you a dead man." Asher's voice is cold.

My pussy turns into fucking Niagara Falls.

Is that supposed to be sexy? Because, oh my hell, it is.

Rio digs into the man's pocket, pulls out his wallet, and takes a picture of his ID. He hands the wallet back, and the man snatches it from Rio's grasp. "Enjoy your hands while you still have them."

The man scrambles on his ass away from us. "You don't know who you're messing with!"

Rio fakes contemplation and places a finger on his chin. "Hmm. Interesting. But we don't give a fuck." Then shrugs his shoulders.

"We'll give you a head start. Use it wisely," Asher adds.

The man finally gives in to his fight-or-flight response—he chooses flight.

I bite my lip when they all turn to me. Their anger turns to lust when they take in my flushed, needy complexion.

"Come on, Mama. Let's go." Rio takes my hand in his and leads us out of the club. Night has settled in, but it's impossible to tell with all the lights of the city.

As we walk to the car, I tilt my head to the side as a question pops into my head. "What happened to the guy from Moonlit?"

Zane's confused expression fails to convince me he doesn't remember. Rio frowns and shrugs a shoulder.

"What guy?" Asher questions.

Rio gives Asher the information he wants. "There was another guy who put his hands on our girlfriend—"

"Before I was your girlfriend," I interject.

"Angel, you were always ours. From the moment I saw you, I knew it."

"The rest was just formalities." Rio waves his hand.

"Don't fight it, Princess. You won't win this argument."

I sigh and roll my eyes at their nonsense.

You know it's true.

Ah, fuck. Yeah, I know.

"What the hell is that?" Zane squints his eyes as we approach his car.

They all draw their weapons when I finally see the manilla envelope on Zane's windshield. Asher reaches the envelope first and opens it while Zane and Rio scan up and down the street.

Asher pulls out multiple photos and a written note. "Fuck!" he shouts, making me jump.

Rio leans in, and all the blood drains from his face. Zane peeks at the images and swallows.

"What is it?" I finally question.

Asher silently hands me everything.

"Oh my God!" I gasp and cover my mouth. The pictures are of Carmen—she's tied with duct tape to a chair. Her face is stained with tear streaks and her eyes are staring right at me, begging for help. I flip through the photos until I get to the note.

The whore for my Flower. Tomorrow at Euphoria 10 p.m.. Come alone.

Anthony is never going to stop. I've always known that. I thought I could run and hide, hoping the problem would go away, but he's not going to stop.

Not until I put a bullet between his eyes.

CHAPTER 24

ZANE

My foot presses the gas pedal to the floor, speeding down the street. I honk my horn in warning, and pedestrians jump out of the way. The stench of burning rubber fills the air as I weave around inexperienced drivers and insistent taxis.

"Come on. Pick up the goddamn phone!" Rio calls Gabriel repeatedly. He won't give up until he answers.

"Maybe he's busy?" Spencer suggests from the backseat.

"We can't count on the MS-13. We need to make our plans without them," Asher vocalizes.

I know Rio doesn't want it to be true—he wants Gabriel to tell him that Carmen is safe at home. I'm sure he'll even settle for her being safe in Gabriel's bed. We may not like them together, but at least we would know she's not with a serial killer and his fucking lapdog.

The Flores family has always given me what I didn't have growing up in the foster system: a familial bond. Carmen never needed a moment to adjust to having two new men in her life when Asher and I entered the picture. She's always had a quiet strength and a hidden fiery side that only rears its head occasionally.

Spencer reaches for Rio, offering him comfort. "It'll be okay. I'll—"

"Don't you dare say it," Rio snaps.

"I'll do it. I'll give myself to him if it means Carmen gets to go home," Spencer insists.

Like hell. Fuck that.

Asher practically jumps out of his seat next to Spencer. "Abso- fucking-lutely not!"

"That's not happening, Angel."

"But—"

"No." Rio's voice emits finality. "I will not trade my girlfriend for my sister. They don't get to force me to make that choice."

Carmen may not be my sister by blood, but she's might as well be.

But Rio's right. Anthony and Pierce don't get to dictate the terms here. This city is our home. These are our lives. They won't get away with attempting to manipulate us like puppets.

Asher argues our point further. "And there's no guarantee that Anthony will hand over Carmen once he has you—he's most likely lying. The risk is too high. We'll figure out something else."

"But Carmen—"

"We'll get her back, Princess." Asher places his arm across Spencer's shoulders. The guilt is written across her face, but this isn't her fault. Only one party is to blame.

"Fucking finally!" Rio pulls the phone away from his ear and puts it on speaker.

"What's going on, *hombre*?" Gabriel asks.

I glare at the road just after hearing Gabriel's voice. "You're not asking the questions here, wannabe gangster."

"Ahh, Detective Kingston. Good to hear from you." His greeting is full of sarcasm. He's still pissed that I arrested his cousin.

Cry me a river, dickface.

Rio ignores Gabriel's question. "Where's Carmen?"

Gabriel tries to sound affronted. "Why do you assume she's with me?"

"*No soy estúpido.* I know there's something going on with you, your minions, and my sister." *I'm not stupid.*

Gabriel sighs. "She said she needed space while she studied for her big test."

Rio scoffs. "There's no way *you* actually left her without someone watching."

"Carmen said we were overbearing and made some pretty good arguments to make her point, so we agreed to back off for a minute."

Rio shakes his head. "You mean she threatened to never speak to you again."

Carmen has always been too smart for her own good. When she chose to follow in Rio's footsteps to become a prosecutor, he was proud. Even if we know that office is corrupt, Carmen will clean it up.

"Something like that." I can hear Gabriel's eye roll through the phone.

She's too good for you, asshole. Choke on it.

I'm not Gabriel's biggest fan. Never have been and never will be.

"I answered your questions. Now you can answer mine." Gabriel's tone shifts from sister's boyfriend to MS-13 *palabrero.* "What. The. Fuck. Happened."

Rio doesn't give Gabriel the information he wants. "Meet us at Spencer's apartment in Chelsea. I know you know where it is." He hangs up without waiting for Gabriel to confirm.

"He could be in on it," I speculate.

"He's not," Rio insists.

My lips flatten into a firm line. "You don't know that."

"Yes, I do." Rio stands strong in his belief.

"How?"

Rio snaps his cold hard eyes to me. "Because he looks at her the way we look at Spencer."

CHAPTER 25

SPENCER

*P*ushing aside the guilt building in my stomach is difficult, but I can't let my guys worry about the stupid shit I might do right now. I will never admit to them that attempting to run was a mistake.

I may be remorseful, but I also have pride.

Anthony did this. Anthony is to blame—not me. Zane's driving has never given me pause, but I might throw up in his backseat. The erratic back and forth motion makes me feel like I'm on a boat in the middle of a hurricane.

When we finally arrive at my apartment, we jump out of the car and sprint inside. We maneuver around each other, stripping off our clothes and changing into practical attire. I look at each of us after we're dressed and chuckle.

Great timing, genius.

They all freeze.

Zane's brows draw together. "What's so funny?"

Asher looks to Zane and Rio. "Is she going into shock?"

"Should we grab towels?" Rio asks.

Asher frowns. "Why the hell would we need towels for this?"

Rio throws his hands up in the air. "They're always grabbing towels when something happens in movies!"

Zane shakes his head, and I laugh harder.

"No, no. I'm fine, I swear." I roll my lips to keep the laugh inside but fail. My abs become sore, and I hold my stomach, bending at the waist. "Y'all look so—"

Their hands guide me to stand upright.

"What?" Zane is getting more and more concerned by the second.

"Y'all look so adorable in your matching outfits."

Asher grimaces, and Zane blinks rapidly while Rio has a smug look on his face. They're wearing black cargo pants with multiple pockets on each leg, muscle black tees that hug their sculpted bodies, and black combat boots. All are clearly from the same store.

Bad Guys 'R' Us. Must be a members-only store.

Asher accuses Rio. "You did this, didn't you?"

Rio doesn't deny it and lifts a shoulder.

Zane pinches the bridge of his nose. "You would."

"You two wouldn't let me give us a name, so I figured the next best thing was matching mission costumes," Rio defends himself.

My eyebrows shoot up. "Y'all have a name?"

"No," Asher and Zane bellow in unison.

"Only because you buzzkills made sure of that," Rio grumbles and crosses his arms.

I know we need to be serious, but whatever I can do to bring them a little light while we wait for Gabriel to get here, I'll do it. "Let me hear some."

"Don't encourage him," Asher implores me.

Rio ignores him and turns to me. Excitement enters his eyes. "The Devil's Sword."

My face scrunches. "Veto."

Rio doesn't let my rejection of the name stop him. "The Henchmen, The Devil's Army . . ."

"We vetoed those already," Asher interjects.

"The Devil's Errand Boys," Rio continues.

I shake my head. "That sounds like a weird boy band."

"Please stop," Zane whines.

"The Devils of New York."

Tilting my head, I respond. "Ooo! That has a nice ring to it."

Rio claps his hands. "Our queen has spoken!"

Asher and Zane groan.

Rio quite literally looks like a kid in a candy store. "I'll add you to our group chat."

I mock frown. "Don't I get a matching outfit too?"

Rio smirks. "Check your closet."

He didn't . . .

But you know he totally would.

Rio beats me to it and hands over my very own badass outfit. They leave me alone to put it on and move to the kitchen. When I'm done, I look at my reflection in the mirror. I'm not the same woman I was a couple of months ago—she wouldn't recognize me.

As I enter the kitchen, they all turn to me. Asher's expression is one of pride, Rio's is seductive, and Zane's is admiration.

Before we can exchange words, there's a pounding on the door. The weight of tonight returns as we all feel the pressure return to our shoulders.

Rio opens the door. "You're late."

Gabriel swaggers in, followed by Diego and Mateo. "I didn't know there was a time constraint, *amigo*."

Mateo spots me and winks, intentionally trying to ruffle some feathers. Diego scans the room, committing every detail to memory.

"Why don't we all sit down," I suggest, motioning to the large couch.

Gabriel's eyes turn calculating and he smirks. "It's nice to know someone here still has some manners." He crosses the open room to the couch and takes a seat on the cushion closest to the door. Diego and Mateo don't sit, and instead spread out, taking up sentry strategically in the space. Zane and Asher take up position next to Diego and Mateo. Rio grabs the manilla envelope from the counter and follows me as I sit on the sectional a few feet from Gabriel.

No one speaks for a solid minute. In silence, they exchange threats I'm sure they've made countless times.

This gangster act is frankly annoying.

"Okay, that's enough," I snap. "If you need a measuring tape to make this go faster, I have one downstairs in my studio. But if we can skip past that part and get to the part where we decide how to rescue Carmen, that'd be convenient."

Mateo and Diego react instantly. Gabriel keeps his composure, but his eyes give him away. He's freaking out.

I figured they didn't know, but now it's confirmed.

"What are you talking about?" Mateo grills.

"Where is she?" Diego's voice borders on the line of anger and desperation.

My men struggle to get the words out—I don't blame them. Rio has been here before, and it didn't have a happy ending.

I sit up taller and grab the envelope out of Rio's hands, tossing it to Gabriel. "It's all there. We need your help getting her back."

"We don't need them," Zane comments.

"Yes, we do," I push back.

When neither Asher nor Rio agrees with Zane, I know I'm right. I've never planned something like this before, but even I know we can't do this on our own. It was a miracle that Rio and Zane were able to pull off that rescue without getting a scratch on them.

Gabriel scrunches his brows as he empties the contents onto his lap. The pictures fall, and Mateo's and Diego's eyes drop to the pictures, clearly on display.

"*Ay dios mio*," Mateo whispers. *Oh my God.*

Diego's face turns red.

Gabriel takes his time examining each photo and reading the note. He keeps his face empty of emotion, but his hands shake with suppressed rage. When he's done, he places everything back in the envelope. "We'll take care of it."

"Fuck no," Asher barks.

"Not without us," Zane protests.

"That's my sister!" Rio moves to stand, but I place my hand on his shoulder, urging him to sit back down.

Guess it's up to me to be the rational one.

"You won't get far without us," I inform Gabriel.

He scoffs. "What? Are you going to throw some clay at them?" His ridicule is just a way to mask his fear.

We all hide our fear because it can make us weak and vulnerable. People are easily manipulated when they're in that state. Most of us know what it's like to trust someone when we're scared, only to be taken advantage of. One hurt soul can easily recognize another.

I don't play into Gabriel's game by reacting to his barbed words. "If you try to negotiate with Anthony without me there, he'll kill you on the spot."

Gabriel leans toward me, resting his elbows on his knees. "I don't give a fuck what happens to me."

"He'll kill Carmen too. He has no qualms about killing whoever he needs to get me back. We have to work together on this. Anthony has money, and lots of it. He can buy whatever and whoever. You go there without us, and you might as well shoot Carmen yourself."

Gabriel rests his fist against his mouth as he stares at me, thinking over what I've said. I keep my hands still, not wanting him to see me flinch.

"Fine. What do you have in mind?"

CHAPTER 26

CARMEN

*L*ight music floats into the back seat. On either side of me sits an intimidating asshole. They're dressed like they were Secret Service in a former life, but they don't act like it.

I'm unable to control the quiver of my shoulders.

I was studying for the LSATs on campus late at night when a cloth was placed over my mouth and nose. In my panic, I inhaled a sickly-sweet odor, then my vision went dark, and when I woke up, I was in a musky warehouse. The men on either side of me now were there, leering at my body. They held me at gunpoint and made me strip off all my clothes. I was treated like an object as Anthony told them to check to see if my virginity was still intact. It's not, but they wouldn't take my word for it. Then, every inch of my body was examined.

Afterward, I was allowed to dress, and I tried to run—I didn't get far and paid for my attempt. My clothes were torn in the struggle, and my nose smacked against the concrete floor, causing it to bleed. I was thrown into a chair, and they tied me to it with duct tape. All while their bosses watched in amusement.

The man driving the car now said his name was Pierce, and he told me to thank Spencer for my current situation. I still don't know what to make of that, but I know she didn't set me up for this. There's no way Spencer would do something like that. If she did, my brother wouldn't be dating her.

The other man, Anthony, treats me like I'm a means to an end.

They've told me their names and haven't made an effort to hide their faces. It doesn't take a genius to know what that means . . .

They don't plan on letting me survive this.

Hopefully, by now, Rio, Asher, and Zane have noticed I'm missing and are coming for me. I made Gabriel, Mateo, and Diego give me space, so I doubt they know about my kidnapping.

"Where are you taking me?"

Anthony turns in his seat like he's planning on giving me an answer when they've ignored my questions thus far. He rears his hand back and brings it across my face. My head whips to the side, and the coppery taste of blood fills my mouth. Involuntary tears sting the corners of my eyes.

"Keep your mouth shut, you low-life whore," Anthony spits at me.

My hand instinctively raises to my cheek, and the skin there heats up.

Anthony looks to the assholes with me in the backseat. "After she's served her purpose, you can do what you want with her . . . and make sure it hurts."

I look back and forth between the two men. The one on my right licks his lips as his eyes rake over my skin. The other stares at my breasts while he adjusts the erection in his pants.

I make myself as small as possible and do as Anthony says.

I remain silent for the rest of the drive.

This isn't the first time someone has used their muscle to beat me down—it may not even be the last—but it's the last time I'll take it lying down.

I'M FORCED from the car when one of the creeps drags me out by my hair. I bite my lip hard to prevent myself from crying out. The muscled creeps grab my arms, and we walk behind Anthony and Pierce as we near a brown brick building in Yonkers. I note the lack of windows.

There's another man who looks identical to my two prison guards at the black metal door. He opens it for us, and the scent of booze, smoke, and sex fills my nose. Music pounds against my eardrums, and I'm hauled inside.

The hallway we enter is dark, and the air is stale. We go through another door with another man standing guard, and light finally meets my eyes. I blink, adjusting to the stage lights as I'm forced to cross to the far side of the main area, but no one pays attention to us.

To the right is a bar with liquor shelves lining the entire wall. There's a large stage opposite the bar with a silver pole. A topless blonde woman in a G-string dances seductively as men in suits sit in red armchairs that line the edge of the stage. She gives each one attention, and they respond in kind by sticking bills in her thong or tossing them on the stage. There are two smaller stages also surrounded by cushy armchairs. One woman occupies each mini stage, and each woman has a full audience.

Anthony nods to a door that says "Employees Only" as he and Pierce head up a set of stairs hidden behind the bar.

"Get ready," one of my guards tells me as he shoves me through the door. I fall to all fours on ugly white tile. My palms sting and I can feel bruises forming on my knees.

"Better yet, stay just like that. Easier access." They chuckle together and a chill races down my spine.

I flip and scramble backwards to get away from them. A set of gentle hands land on my shoulders. Looking up, I find a woman with long, black hair and deep blue eyes. She is scantily dressed in a bra and panties, but she doesn't act embarrassed whatsoever. Instead, the threat of violence in her eyes is directed at the men who pushed me in here.

The men smirk and one says, "Good to see you, Raven. Dancing tonight?"

Her vein at her temple pulses. "You know I am, Jared, or else I wouldn't be here."

"Ah, ah, ah. Watch your tone or I'll make sure you don't make your quota tonight."

Raven clenches her jaw to stop herself from responding. Jared gives her a disgusting smirk and shuts the door. A deadbolt slides into place, locking us inside with no way out.

Raven helps me to my feet, and I look around the room.

We're not alone.

There are clothing racks at the back and vanities all over the place. Most of them are occupied by women who are similarly dressed to Raven. They're all watching us.

I also note that there isn't a second door.

No way out.

"Are you okay?" Raven questions me.

"I'll be fine."

Fake it 'til you make it.

"What's your name, honey?"

"Carmen," I answer.

She places an arm around me and guides me to an empty vanity, sitting me in the chair. "Let's get you dressed. They're going to expect you to be ready when they come back to escort you to the stage."

My jaw drops as I stare at her in disbelief through the mirror. "The stage?"

The corners of Raven's lips turn up in sympathy. "That's how it works. They usually make the girls that they don't want to get roughed up by their usual clientele dance."

A pit forms in my stomach. "Usual clientele?"

"These men are in the skin trade—we're nothing more than cattle to them. We get to live as long as we make them money, and they put us wherever they can capitalize on us. It's either the streets, the sheets, or the pole."

I refuse to let my tears fall. I refuse to let my fear show.

"Do you have any kids?" Raven inquires.

"Umm. No." I shake my head.

"Good. They'll use your children against you."

My heart falls. "Is that what they did to you?"

Her deep blue irises look hopeless. "Yeah. They have my son, Noah. He's how they keep me from running away." She's given up hope.

My breathing picks up. "I can't do this." This can't be my life now.

"Just do what they want, and you'll be fine."

This can't be how I live the rest of my life.

I don't know if anyone is looking for me.

I have to be my own hero.

CHAPTER 27

SPENCER

Saying that I have butterflies in my stomach isn't accurate. It's more like my stomach feels as if it wants to fold into a ball of goop and venture outside of my body.

After the seven of us finished scheming, we set about getting everything in order to execute our plan. Gabriel, Mateo, and Diego left to gather their people even though Zane wasn't too keen on involving other members of the MS-13 because they've shown that they can be bought.

We were all tense as we waited through the night and all day. We didn't talk much, we just existed in the same space together. When it finally comes time to leave, we pile into the mobile bat cave.

Rio and Zane are supposed to wait in the van while Asher and I go inside Euphoria. The note said to come alone, but none of my men were willing to comply with those demands. Asher insisted on being the one in there with me in case bullets start flying.

Gabriel, Mateo, and Diego are supposed to be there already. Their job is to blend into the audience and find out where they're holding Carmen. Once they know, they're supposed to let Rio and Zane know. From there, Rio and Zane are to cause some type of distraction outside the building to draw attention. Then we're supposed to find an exit. MS-13 members are supposed to be standing by in case we need help.

"Everything's going to be okay," Rio tries to reassure me. He pulls me close, and we rest our heads together. We breathe together, basking in our connection.

Rio's phone vibrates in his pocket, breaking the moment. He pulls out his phone and reads his screen, furrowing his brows. "They found Carmen already," he apprises us.

"What?"

"How?"

"Where is she?"

"*Mierda*. She's on stage."

Fucking hell. This just got more complicated.

ASHER KEEPS a hand on my back as we walk down the sidewalk in the dark of night. Beads of sweat form at my temples from the summer heat. Rio and Zane dropped us off a block away while they drove closer to the club to park and wait for our signal.

"We got this."

I peek at Asher. "Are you trying to comfort me or yourself?"

"Both, I guess." He shrugs.

At least he's honest.

We're stopped at the door where one of Anthony and Pierce's henchmen stands guard. "I need to pat you down."

"Over my dead body," Asher maneuvers so his body shields mine.

"No one gets in without being checked." The guard doesn't budge.

I place my hand on Asher's arm. "Hey, big guy, it's okay."

He gives me a skeptical look over his shoulder, and I give him a half-smile in return. Stepping forward, Asher goes first. The guard removes Asher's guns and magazines hidden under his jacket. When it's my turn, the guard finds the throwing knives, handgun, extra magazines, pocketknife, pepper spray, and the rape whistle.

My guys loaded me up before we left my apartment. I didn't even try to argue because I knew it made them feel better.

The guard gives me a judgmental look as he glances back and forth between me and my pile of weapons, but I ignore him.

Once he's satisfied that we're no longer armed, he opens the door, granting us entry. Another guard escorts us through a dark hallway and into the club.

Game time.

Masking my emotions has never been my strong suit, but I would walk barefoot across broken glass to save Carmen. I can do this.

The bright lights and heavy bass music fill the room. I spot Carmen right away.

Carmen is handcuffed to the pole on a small stage in across the room.

She's in sky-high heels, a lacy push-up bra, and a thong. Her makeup is perfect and dramatic, and her hair hangs in natural waves down her back. Her cuffed hand clutches the pole as she walks in a circle around it. Carmen doesn't bother to put any effort into trying to dance to the music.

We lock gazes, and her lips part in silent surprise. Her eyes bounce back and forth between Asher and me.

Explaining everything is going to be a fun *conversation.*

A row of chairs surround Carmen's circular stage, but only two are occupied. Anthony and Pierce lounge in their seats, ignoring her forced performance. They track my every step toward them.

Carmen discreetly glances at Diego who sits at the bar. Mateo is in an armchair at the main stage, where a gorgeous woman with black hair spins around on the pole. Gabriel lounges in another chair in front of the other small stage, where a woman with red curly hair removes her clothes for the customers.

Anthony stands from his seat and rounds the edge of the stage while Pierce remains seated. There are two more men stationed behind them. The bulge of their guns is visible beneath their expensive black suits.

"You're dismissed." Anthony waves his hand, indicating that the men should leave us, but he doesn't look away from me as he says it. He makes a point to ignore Asher's presence, but he can't help it when he's been defied. "You were supposed to come alone, Flower."

"We can't always get what we want," I retort and cross my arms. Holding my chin high, I refuse to flinch.

Anthony's condescending laugh has a sharp edge. "I do. Every time." He looks me up and down. "I got you."

I dig my fingers into the skin of my arms as I keep myself from acting on impulse and punching Anthony's throat.

Coming face to face with the man who has hurt me for years and knowing the full story, I feel this urge to start swinging my fists. But we have a plan, and if I want everyone to make it out alive, then I need to follow that plan.

"You *purchased* me. There's a difference."

Anthony grips my chin roughly and steps close. "I was the

one to take your virgin pussy. I still remember what your innocent blood looked like on my dick."

Fuming, my lips tighten into a stubborn line. "Again. *Purchased.*"

"It seems you already forgot my lesson. I'll be happy to teach you again, though. Don't you worry." Anthony's smile is full of malice. "And what do you think you're wearing? You look ridiculous. Are you auditioning for a G.I. Jane role?"

I raise a brow. "I actually like this outfit. I'm thinking about making this my new look."

Anthony's fingers dig into my skin. "You need to watch the way you talk to me, Flower."

Asher's breathing is deep, and the vein in his neck pulses dangerously fast. His gaze is locked on Anthony's hand. The longer he stares, the closer he seems to get to breaking Anthony's fingers one by one.

"Run along, Agent," Anthony dismisses Asher, and another guard approaches Asher, grabbing his arm.

Asher roots himself in place and yanks his arm away. "I'm not leaving without Carmen."

"Ah, yes." Anthony turns his head so Pierce can hear him. "Help our guest down, won't you, Pierce?"

Pierce looks affronted. "Why me?"

Anthony doesn't enjoy the questioning of his authority. He goes rigid and commands, "Just do it, Pierce."

Pierce gulps down the rest of his drink and slams the glass down on the side table. A dribble of alcohol trickles from the corner of his mouth, and he swipes it away with the back of his hand.

How graceful.

He jumps up onto the stage, bypassing the steps, and removes a key from his pocket. Pierce's grip around Carmen's wrist is visibly too tight as he uses the key to remove the handcuffs, but Carmen doesn't let the pain show as she glances at the bar again, subtly shaking her head.

"Come on. Big brother gave up his bitch to get you back. Time to go." He shoves Carmen off the stage in our direction. As she falls, she lands on her side and hits her head on the ground. He hops down, bending his knees to brace himself, and lands beside Anthony. He squats down next to Carmen and whispers something else in her ear.

Carmen's cheeks flame, and she lifts her head and spits right in Pierce's face. Pierce rears his hand back and smacks her across the face. The force causes Carmen to fall back down.

Anthony drops his grip on my chin and leans his head to the side. I follow his line of sight, and my breath catches in my throat.

Shit.

With guns in hand, Gabriel, Diego, and Mateo sprint towards Carmen. Anthony draws his handgun from his waist while Pierce and their men do the same.

My heart stops as Anthony raises his gun and fires.

CHAPTER 28

GABRIEL

My fingers tap on the arm of my chair as I set my chin against my fist on the other arm. A beautiful redhead dances on the stage in front of me, but my attention is transfixed on the woman who has unwittingly enchanted me.

I knew the moment I brought her into my life I was putting her in danger. But Carmen Flores isn't a fragile snowflake.

She's a spitfire. She's fierce.

Even now. She's nearly naked in a room full of people. She has been kidnapped and hurt, but her pride is intact, and she holds her head high. As she walks around the pole in her heels, she rolls her eyes at the two men sitting by her stage.

That's my girl.

Carmen's acting like she has chewed gum on her shoe rather than acting like she's been kidnapped by human traffickers.

The two men, Anthony Cole and Pierce Murphy, laugh together at Carmen's annoyance. They're going to regret taking what's ours.

My eyes wander to the main stage, where Mateo pretends to be entertained by the dancer there. He puts his index and middle fingers together and touches his lips with them. Slyly switching my attention to the bar, Diego gives me the same sign.

They're both ready.

Asher and Spencer walk in with one of Anthony and Pierce's men. The man walks with false *machismo*. He thinks his big gun makes him tough.

Idiota.

As they walk by, Asher looks at me and nods his head once.

Another step closer to getting Carmen out of here.

I need her back where she belongs. In my home, my bed—fuck giving her space. We gave her space, and this happens.

I watch as Spencer, Asher, and Anthony talk together. They may not be throwing punches, but they're close to it. The way Spencer clutches her arms and the way Asher's muscles in his back are taut tell me all I need to know.

As Pierce jumps up onto the stage right next to Carmen, I sit forward in my seat. My hand rests on the gun hidden under my suit jacket.

Pierce produces a key and unlocks the handcuffs. Once she's free, he pushes her off the stage and onto the floor. Carmen doesn't have time to brace for the fall, and she lands on her side.

He was already a dead man, but now he's going to suffer.

Jumping to my feet, I watch them intensely. In my peripheral vision, I notice Diego and Mateo standing as well. Pierce hops down and crouches beside Carmen.

Don't be stupid, mi vida.

"Do you need a refill, sir?" A waitress with oversized wild hair and fake boobs presses her cleavage against my arm.

"No." I don't even glance in her direction.

"Let me know if there's *anything* I can help you with." Her finger drags down my sleeve in an attempt at seduction.

"Not likely."

She pouts but accepts my answer and walks away.

Whatever Pierce says to Carmen sets her off. Her eyes glow with her wrath, and she spits right in his face. Pierce doesn't even wipe his face before his hand is ready to fly.

Fuck this. I'm not waiting.

I whip out my piece and sprint across the floor to Carmen. Diego and Mateo move with me, but we don't reach them before Pierce slaps Carmen across the face. She falls back to the floor, and her hand goes to her cheek.

That's another month of pain for this cabrón.

Anthony notices us coming and shoves Spencer aside while drawing his gun. Asher grabs Spencer and throws her to the floor while he lays on top to protect her.

As Anthony takes aim and begins to fire, we don't stop running to them. His first shot goes high, and the second goes too wide.

Screams erupt around us, and people begin to run in every direction to leave Euphoria. Anthony and Pierce's men all leave their posts and converge on us, firing their guns as well. Diego, Mateo, and I shoot back, taking down a few of them.

Anthony continues shooting as he moves backwards toward a set of hidden stairs. Spencer spots him attempting to flee and elbows Asher in the stomach to get him off her. When she's free, she takes off after Anthony, swiping a gun from a dead guard.

"Spencer! Don't you dare!" Asher shouts. He leaps to his feet and chases Spencer, pilfering a gun of his own on his way.

La mara hears the gunshots and comes running from where they've been lying in wait. As they enter, their guns are drawn and aimed at the men firing at us. A full-blown shoot-out ensues.

Rio and Zane enter behind *la mara*. We make eye contact for a split second, and I point to the stairs, letting them know where to find Asher and Spencer. They don't miss a step as they dart to the staircase.

"Stay back!" Pierce shouts at us as he makes Carmen stand with him and holds his gun to her temple.

For the first time in a long time, my hands sweat, and a sickening wave of terrors builds low in my stomach.

But we don't stop.

My focus is stuck on the barrel of the gun aimed at the woman who has my heart—*all* our hearts.

Carmen keeps her mouth shut as the gun is pressed further into her skin. Her breathing is visible as her chest moves up and down dramatically. Her eyes are wide, and tears well in her eyes.

Our guns are all pointed at Pierce, and I'm ready to pull the trigger. He won't be the first man I've killed, and he won't be the last.

"I said stay back!" Pierce's hand shakes as he backs away in a different direction than the one Anthony took.

"Not going to happen, *pendejo*!" Mateo shouts back.

"It's okay, Teo. D, step back." Carmen's voice quivers. "Gabe, look at me. I'll be fine."

We don't listen. We can't walk away.

"Listen to her, you bastards! Back off!" Pierce's voice ascends into a murderous falsetto. His crazed eyes dart around the room as he realizes there's nothing he can do to make us leave. Desperation closes in on him from all sides.

Pierce swings his gun in our direction and fires aimlessly. We can't shoot back—we would risk hitting Carmen.

Diego yells as a bullet grazes his arm. Mateo and I turn to

jump on top of Diego. I make it one step before a burning fire pierces my stomach. My hand automatically covers the spot where the pain seems to be coming from. When I look down at my hand, it's covered in red.

"No!" Carmen screeches. Her heart is in her scream.

I look at her and find the worry in her eyes. She struggles to get free and fails. So, she reaches behind her and rakes her nails down Pierce's face.

Pierce cries out, "Fucking whore!" Then he pushes Carmen to the floor and opens the door behind him to a hallway we didn't know was there. He points his gun down and gets off two rounds. Without glancing back, he runs down the hall, and the door swings shut behind him.

Carmen lies on the floor motionless.

CHAPTER 29

SPENCER

I'm familiar with the sounds of gunfire—I'll never forget what it's like to have bullets flying all around me.

This time around is just as bad as the first.

The *pop, pop, pop* of rapid gunfire echoes all around the room.

The suffocating vice of fear is not so easy to disregard, but I won't let it keep me from finishing this.

Asher covers my body with his own, but I'm still able to lift my head. When I do, I spot Anthony walking backwards toward the stairs and wildly firing his gun.

He can't get away again.

Ramming my elbow into Asher's gut three times in rapid succession, I roll him off me. His groan meets my ears, but only a smidge of guilt drops on my shoulders. I push up from my stomach and chase after Anthony. As I run by a dead body, I snatch the gun from his still hand.

"Spencer! Don't you dare!"

Asher's threat is empty, and I don't falter as I race up a set of metal stairs. Heavy footsteps follow me, but I don't need to check to know it's Asher.

The door at the top is open a sliver, but that's all I need.

Using the barrel of my gun, I slowly push open the door and hold my breath.

"I think the fuck not, Princess," Asher harshly whispers behind me. "I go in first." He easily moves me aside and takes my place at the entry of the door.

Asher slowly opens the door, but the door blocks our view of the rest of the room. We haven't even stepped into the room when bullets break through the door.

"Fuck!" Asher swears as he moves us back onto the stairs. He takes a deep breath, kicks the door open the rest of the way, and dives into the room. He takes cover behind a bar cart littered with expensive alcohol, and I keep my spot behind the open door.

"Asher!" My heart stops as I hear more discharged bullets hit the wall and floor in our direction.

Peeking around the door, I memorize everything I see and fire my gun two times. A large mahogany desk sits in the middle of the room. A black leather couch is situated against the wall, and two black leather chairs are placed in front of the desk.

One more peek.

More bullets.

One wall is a large window that looks down on the main floor of Euphoria. There's a large metal door at the opposite end of the room.

Glass and wood splinters rain down on us as Asher and I take turns firing our guns in Anthony's direction.

During a pause, Anthony shouts, "If you come with me now, Spencer, I will walk away, and I won't kill your little playthings."

Anthony's offer appeals to a part of me that feels helpless.

This side of myself is tired. She's done fighting for every happy moment and every positive thought. She wants to give up and give in. If I agree to go, then everyone I love will be safe.

But the side that has gotten louder over the last several weeks protests loudly. She reminds me of the happiness and security I've felt with my men. She isn't willing to give into the demands of someone so entitled that they take whenever they want without thinking of the consequences.

"When hell freezes over!" I answer and resume shooting. Asher joins back in, and Anthony takes his turn as well.

After only a couple of minutes, all our guns click. Our magazines are empty.

Fucking hell.

Asher's head pops up from behind the cart, I peer around the door, and Anthony pokes his head up from behind the solid desk.

Anthony sees me and smirks.

My breaths billow through my teeth, and my face turns crimson.

That asshole just shot at me and my boyfriend.

Vengeance isn't some abstract idea—it isn't some unattainable dream. Vengeance is right here in front of me, and it's mine to take.

Asher reads me like an open book. "No, Princess."

I lock my jaw and move my head from side to side. Not waiting for another protest from Asher, I bolt straight to the desk where Anthony stands, waiting for me.

Anthony opens his mouth to speak, but I don't let him get a word in. I crawl on top of the desk, and when he opens his mouth, I punch him right in the throat. He chokes and grabs at his neck, falling back into the office chair behind him.

"You don't get to say anything!" I scream. "You took too much from me!"

Hands grab at my shoulders and arms from behind me.

"Angel, just back away."

"Let us help, Mama."

"We can take care of this for you, Princess."

Pulling away, I jump on top of Anthony and allow my fists to rain down on his face. I feel the presence of my men come up behind me, but this time they don't interfere.

Blood pours from Anthony's nose, and the skin on his cheek breaks. When he finally makes an effort to fight back, Asher, Rio, and Zane grab Anthony's arms and legs, holding them in place.

Punch. Jab.

Packing my car and fleeing Houston.

Punch. Jab.

Starting my life in a new place and making my own family.

Punch. Jab.

Meeting three amazing men who helped me live again.

"Spencer. Angel."

Punch. Jab.

"Princess."

"Mama."

Punch. Jab.

I'm lifted off Anthony, and I flail my limbs wildly. "Let me go! Let me go!"

"That's enough. You're hurting yourself more than him at this point." Asher's inked, strong arms remain wrapped around my middle.

Taking in a breath, I calm my pounding heart and examine my now-aching fists. They're covered in the same amount of blood that covers Anthony's face.

So much red.

"I'm okay," I reassure everyone. "I'm okay."

Asher sets me back on my feet while Zane and Rio stand guard over Anthony. His eyes are so swollen that I'm sure he can barely see the room anymore. Bruises are scattered all over his face. He groans and his head droops forward.

"What do you want to do next?" Rio inquires.

I give him a confused look. "What do you mean?"

Zane answers me. "It's your choice what we do with him. We can turn him over to the police, or . . ."

"Or?"

Asher rests his hands on my shoulder in support. "Or you can end it all yourself. Right here, right now."

Zane hands over his gun, placing it in my hands. I stare down at the complex, small machine.

Am I ready to live with someone's death on my hands?

The simple answer is yes, I am more than ready and willing to take on the burden. Although, for someone like Anthony, it's more like a public service.

I wrap my hand around the cool metal of the grip, feeling the weight of the whole thing in my palm. Looking up, I nod to Zane and Rio. They push Anthony onto the floor on his knees.

"Are you really going to kill me, Flower?" Anthony's question is slurred, and he spits out a glob of blood at my feet.

"Yes," I state coldly. "You have too many people in office under your thumb. You'd either escape prison, or you'd live it up on the inside. So, I am more than happy to take on the responsibility of being your judge, jury, and executioner."

Anthony scoffs while my men remain stoic and firm.

"Anthony Cole, you are a murderer, a rapist, and a human trafficker. You have purchased hundreds of women and girls, including myself."

He remains kneeling and begins to chuckle.

Grabbing his hair at the top of his head, I pull back so he's looking up at me. "Laugh it up all you want; you're not leaving this room alive."

His smile is wide and bloody. "You don't have the balls."

Leveling the barrel so it points right between his eyes, I breathe. "Try me." I place my finger over the trigger and squeeze. The gun goes off, and brain matter exits the back of Anthony's head. Zane and Rio release their hold on Anthony as he slumps forward and falls onto the carpet.

Am I supposed to feel different right now? Am I supposed to feel guilty? All I feel is relief.

It's over.

All the fight drains from my body at once. Asher removes the gun from my hand and sets it on the desk, and my three men surround me, helping me stand up right when I'm ready to collapse and sleep for the next decade.

"You did good, Angel. You did good."

CHAPTER 30

CARMEN

"¡*Ay dios mio!* You're worse than Rio, Zane, and Asher combined!" Elena and her nurse fuss over me. "You shouldn't even be trying to sit up."

"Calm your tits. *Estoy bien.*" I sigh and rest my head back against the crunchy sanitary pillows.

I'm supposed to be recovering, but how the hell am I supposed to be comfortable when this hospital bed feels like I'm lying on the sidewalk?

"You had emergency surgery to remove a goddamn bullet from your abdomen, and you had two blood transfusions," Elena scolds me like she usually does Mariela. She puts her hands on her hips like the mother I never wanted her to be.

Avoiding eye contact is impossible in my private room. Everywhere I look, there's someone staring at me. Gabriel, Mateo, and Diego hover around my bed while still giving room to the nurse and Elena so they can work. These three men haven't left my hospital room since I woke up. Apparently, they already got their injuries stitched up and don't need to be in hospital beds. I was also told they

184

were here watching me sleep as well. That should be creepy, but their show of affection wraps my heart in a warm blanket.

"You have no idea what it was like, walking into the OR ready to perform surgery on a stranger, only to find you lying there on my table." Elena's lips tremble. "It took three nurses and two doctors just to get me out of the room."

Guilt claws at my throat as I try to swallow it down.

Dammit.

I know it's bad when Elena comes close to tears. My sister has always been tough because she's always had to be. She's the one who taught me about my period while our mother was busy working herself to the bone to keep a roof over our heads. Elena was the one who would make sure I brushed my teeth and would brush my hair.

"You coded in the ambulance, twice," Elena informs me.

"*Lo siento,*" I whisper. *I'm sorry.*

I know it's not my fault—Elena knows it's not my fault. But shock and fear do something strange to us when we come close to losing our loved ones. We all know death is a part of life—you can't have one without the other. But facing that reality is different.

Elena brushes my hair to the side and tucks it behind my ear. "*Nunca me vuelvas a hacer.*" *Don't ever do that to me again.* She leans in, kissing the top of my head, and I hold my tears back. "I'll be back to check on you. And don't you dare think I'm letting you out of here before you fully recover. Your gangster boyfriends can't threaten me into doing shit."

I scoff. "They're not my—"

"Yes, we are," Mateo corrects me before I can contradict Elena.

Elena laughs as she and Nurse Amy exit my room. The silence they leave behind is impossible to navigate.

What does someone say after they've been kidnapped, shot in the stomach, and rescued by their criminal . . . lovers?

"Boyfriends" feels too generous, and what we did together was supposed to be a one-time thing only.

But they did walk through a hailstorm of bullets to rescue me.

Composing my feelings, I put on my "I could care less" face and direct is at Gabriel. "Shouldn't you still be in bed?

To prove a point, Gabriel moves easily across the room and takes the seat closest to me, and scoots the chair all the way forward so he can get right in my face. "Worried about me?" He asks with an arrogant smirk.

Rolling my eyes, I scoff. "Hardly. And to be clear, you three are not my boyfriends."

Gabriel leans in close. Close enough that I can smell the deep manly scent of his skin. "Let's get one thing straight, *mi reina*. You belong to us."

Loud breaths spiral from my nose as my hands ball into fists at my sides. "*You* need to get one thing straight, *hombre*," I reply mockingly. "You can't own me." I emphasize each word by poking his chest.

Gabriel's fingers slide into my hair as he grips the nape of my neck and brings my face closer to his. "I don't want to own you, Carmen. I want to possess you. I want you to know what it's like to be so obsessed with a person that you'd stop breathing when they no longer exist in this world. Your scent haunts me in my sleep. Your body plagues my dreams. My every waking moment is consumed by you. I want you to know what that feels like."

My core clenches around air, hungering to remember what it feels like to be pleasured by these men.

Vulnerability isn't my strong suit, so I don't know why I show it now.

"What makes you think I don't know what that feels like?"

Diego sneers. "You have a funny way of showing it—pushing us away, hiding behind fabricated excuses."

"You don't understand," I attest.

"I think we understand perfectly," Mateo argues back. "We've given you everything you've asked for, and you go and get yourself kidnapped."

I slam my fists down on the bed. "I didn't ask to be kidnapped!"

"Semantics." Mateo waves his hand derisively.

"We're not giving you a choice in this anymore," Gabriel declares in an authoritative tone. "I'm not going to repeat myself again. *Tú nos perteneces.*" *You belong to us.*

Fuck.

This is not going to go well.

CHAPTER 31

ASHER

Extending my feet in front of me, I try to make myself comfortable in the hospital chair. Spencer adjusts with me, leaning her head on my shoulder. Zane sits on the other side of Spencer, her hand in his lap. Rio is trying to portray a calm demeanor, but his arms are crossed and his foot bounces like crazy.

Zane watches Rio with concern. "Elena already told us that Carmen is okay. I'm sure we'll be cleared to see her soon."

"Those *cabróns* get to be in there with her—I don't see why I can't. I'm her damn brother."

We've been in the waiting room for hours while Carmen and fucking Gabriel underwent emergency surgery. When we came down from the office of Euphoria, Rio lost his mind. He went even crazier when we discovered that Pierce had gotten away. Zane called up the NYPD immediately and sent squad cars to all the small local airports, including Teterboro, where we knew Anthony's plane was sitting in a hangar. A BOLO was put out for Pierce, but no dice so far.

The NYPD and FBI are under the impression that we

colluded with the MS-13 to take down a major player and expand MS-13 territory. Only half true, but they'll never figure that out. Our official story is that we went into a hostage situation in which we believed we'd have a better outcome if we didn't involve law enforcement, and the MS-13 just so happened to be there.

Zane and I got angry calls from our superiors. Zane has been suspended for one week, and I have been suspended for two.

Our plan went to shit the moment Pierce put his hands on Carmen. I knew Gabriel, Diego, and Mateo wouldn't be able to hold themselves back for long. But when Spencer surprised me and took off after Anthony, a million different scenarios played through my mind, and none of them ended with Spencer breathing. A huge part of our success is attributed to luck.

Some civilians were killed in the crossfire, but that's the reality of war.

"How are you doing, Princess?"

Spencer peers up at me, a motion that will always make my cock twitch. "Honestly? I'm tired. I want to slip into a medically-induced coma and not wake up for at least a month."

Zane snorts. "Then you better get caffeine in an IV because I have lots of plans for you, and none of them include sleeping."

"They better include foot massages and comfort food," Spencer threatens.

The doors to the waiting room open as Dahlia, Hayes, Kieran, and the three kids step in. Margaret dashes as fast as her small strides can take her straight to Zane and she wraps her arms around his neck. August stands in between Hayes and Dahlia, holding each of their hands. Kieran urges Noah forward gently.

"Did you find my mommy, cop man?" Margaret questions Zane with a head tilt.

"I believe we did. Want me to take you to her?"

Margaret's eyes light up. "She's here? Yes! Yes, please! Now! Let's go now." She scrambles to her feet and drags Zane by his hand out the door.

Spencer approaches Noah calmly. "Your mom is here too. Would you like to see her?"

Noah pinches his lips together as he refrains from letting his tears fall. "Yes, please."

Spencer nods her head and guides Noah out of the waiting room and into the hall. My instinct is to follow her and make sure nothing happens on their short walk to Raven's room, but I hold myself still and soothe my anxiety with the fact that it's over. It's all over.

After all of Anthony and Pierce's men were rounded up, we found all the dancers in a dressing room locked from the outside. Two of them, Raven and Mya, asked about their kids when they finally believed me when I told them that I was FBI and that they were safe.

We ushered them into an ambulance, and Rio demanded that they be taken to St. Barnabas to be treated by Elena. She and her nurse were able to reassure each of the trafficked women that they were safe and free. Many sobbed, some still don't believe us, and a few insisted they be released immediately. The last group was the one with track marks up and down their arms.

Dahlia leads Hayes and August to some chairs on the opposite side of the room and then approaches me. "Is he dead?"

"Yes." I don't need clarification to know who she's talking about.

"Are you sure?"

"Positive. It's over."

She nods her head once, keeping her composure. "Thank you." She turns on her heel and sits with her son.

Rio moves to occupy Spencer's vacated seat. "It's not completely over. We still have one more thing we need to finish."

"I know."

CHAPTER 32

SPENCER

The plane bounces twice on the runway as the pilot lowers us onto the tarmac. Zane's hand squeezes the life out of mine as a bead of sweat drips down the side of his face.

I try to comfort him. "We're okay. We landed safely. No turbulence or anything."

He doesn't respond or even look at me. He just nods and stares wide-eyed at the seat in front of him.

Rio leans over mine and Zane's seats. "He'll be fine, Mama. Zane just doesn't believe that people should fly."

"It's unnatural," Zane defends himself.

"If anyone should be terrified, it's me," Asher chimes in from beside Rio. "These seats were not designed for people of my size."

I snort a small laugh, and Asher shoots me a playful glare.

I've been doing that a lot the last few days—laughing. My men—my devils—have always made me smile, but now there's a new light to the memories we make.

We gather our few things as the flight attendant welcomes us to George Bush Intercontinental Airport. The humidity hits us the moment the cabin door opens, and I can practically hear the entire plane groan. The heat of the day doesn't disappear when the sun goes down and that fact is true tonight as well.

Zane is the first one off the plane and through the Jetway. Rio grabs my hand with Asher behind us as we trail behind Zane.

Rio shakes his head and sighs. "As much as I love you, we're never moving here."

Chuckling, I bump him with my shoulder. "Don't worry. I think I'm a New Yorker at heart."

"You say 'y'all' a lot for a New Yorker," Asher comments under his breath.

"Hey!" I snap back.

We trek with high spirits all the way to arrivals, even with the looming cloud of our agenda today.

Once there, Zane whistles to a man with a sign that reads, "Dickface Kingston." He's about as tall as Zane, with groomed hair that's shorter on the sides and longer on top. When he spots Zane, a smile brightens his face. They hug and exchange pleasantries.

Zane keeps one arm around the man and turns to us. "Griff, you remember Rio and Asher."

"Of course." His response is one that makes me feel like there are stories to tell.

Zane gestures to me. "And this is our girlfriend, Spencer."

Griffin side-eyes Zane playfully. He steps forward with his hand outstretched to me, but when I move to shake his hand, Griffin is yanked back.

"Nice try. Hands to yourself," Zane warns.

Griffin chuckles like a goofy teen. "Can't blame a man for

trying." He holds his hands up as if surrendering to Zane's threat.

"Did you get what we asked for?" Asher inquires.

"Yeah, and I had to call in a lot of favors to make it happen, too," Griffin complains comically. "You know that I'm not an arms dealer or a car dealership, right? And the drive here took a few hours. Just because I live in Texas doesn't mean I zip from one side to another."

Zane doesn't address Griffin's ribbing. "Where's Knox?"

"He's in the parking garage with the car." Griffin tilts his head towards the door.

"Let's get a move on then." Zane slings his duffle and mine over his shoulder, motioning for Griffin to lead the way.

I hang back with Rio on our walk to the parking garage. "How does Zane know this guy?"

"Griffin, his brother, and Zane were in the foster system together for a bit." Rio grabs my hand and interlaces our fingers.

"In Texas?"

"Yeah, Zane bounced from home to home after his foster sister died. He was down here in Texas for a bit because his social worker thought that getting some distance from New Jersey would be good for him."

We approach a blacked-out Ford Bronco with a man who looks identical to Griffin sitting on the hood. His hair is slicked back and longer than Griffin's. He hops down and walks right up to Zane.

Rio reads my confused face and says, "They're twins."

"No shit," I whisper back with all the sass I can muster.

"About time," Knox teases with a small curve of his lips. He's a little more reserved and broodier than Griffin.

"Beauty takes time, Knox," Zane teases back. He shakes

Knox's hand, and they both lean in for a typical bro hug. "Knox, this is Spencer. Spencer, this is Knox—Griffin's twin."

I reach my hand out, and Knox returns the gesture. "Nice to meet you," I greet him.

"Hey! Why does he get to shake her hand, and I don't?" Griffin crosses his arms.

"You know why," Zane deadpans.

Griffin drops his offended act and gestures to the car. "She's all yours. The supplies you requested are in the trunk, and the tank is full."

Knox tosses the keys to Zane, who catches them with one hand. "Thanks, guys."

"No problem! See y'all later." Griffin waves as he and Knox get into a red F-150 and drive away.

"Well, that was fun. Let's get to it." Rio opens the back door and motions for me to get inside. Once I'm settled, he slides in after me while Zane and Asher take their seats in the front.

The drive is easy to the Post Oak Hotel. There's an argument over what music to play, but that's to be expected.

Once we arrive, we park in the Post Oak Hotel parking lot, and Zane turns off the engine.

Looking up at the building, I express my doubt. "Are you sure she's here?"

"Positive," Zane confirms.

"You don't have to do this if you're not ready, Princess." Asher's concern is endearing, but I'm ready for this. I've been ready for this.

My response is to get out of the car and open the back hatch. My men follow me, and I dig around in the canvas bag. I feel the cool steel under my fingertips. I take it out of the bag and check the slide and the magazine, then I screw the silencer on the end.

Rio groans. "Fuck. That was hot."

I shoot Rio a wink. "Let's go."

We follow Asher to the back entrance, where Zane uses a fake keycard to open the door. The stairwell is easy to find, but the ten flights of stairs we have to climb almost kill me.

Before we enter the hall, Zane disables the security cameras. He gives Asher a single nod, letting him know we're good to continue.

Zane opens the door to room number 1016 the same way he opened the back door of the hotel. Asher enters first, as usual, and Rio, Zane, and I follow him. Shopping bags from high end stores are scattered all over the couch and coffee table. Aside from that, the entire suite is empty except for the person sleeping in the bed.

I approach the bed on light feet while Asher, Rio, and Zane stand behind me.

She looks so defenseless like this, almost childlike. But any part of my heart that might take mercy on her was obliterated. She made sure of that.

I flip on the bedside lamp, and she flinches. Her eyes blink and squint as she adjusts to the onslaught of light on her face.

"What the hell?" Mom pushes herself up, resting back on her elbows. Her face flushes red as she realizes who stands around her. "Spencer Lily Gray, you march yourself out of this room right now."

"Tempting offer, but no. I'm here to make sure you answer for your crimes."

"*My* crimes? You're the one in bed with criminals!" Her tone is accusing, but her words float away, missing their target.

"You know what I'm talking about. Don't play dumb, it'll wrinkle your skin." I flash her my gun, and her face goes ghost white.

"I'm sorry, okay? I'm sorry. But . . . what else was I

supposed to do? I was a single mom, and I needed to live. I gave you a good life and found you a wealthy husband. All things considered, you ended up happy. You can walk out of here right now, and I'll forget this ever happened. And take these *thugs* with you, too."

Wrong words, Mom.

Pointing my gun at her head, I tilt my head side to side as if I'm actually giving her statement some thought. "Again, no."

"So, what are you going to do? Arrest me? Good luck trying to prove your claims in court," she mocks.

I feel the silent presence of my men and the strength they give me.

"Unfortunately, that's not the plan." The smile I give her is condescending. "You're not leaving this room tonight. No more shopping sprees. No more rich dumb boyfriends."

"Now, hold a minute—"

"You don't get any last words. I do," I interrupt. Her mouth gapes open and I clear my throat so what I have to say is clear. "Fuck you. Enjoy hell." Then I empty my magazine right into her face.

And she's gone forever.

They say the best vengeance is living well, but shooting the person in the face feels just as good.

Rio whistles as if impressed. "That was gangster, Mama."

I snicker and turn to him. "I'm taking that as a compliment."

"As you should," he quips back.

Asher wraps his arm around me and guides me out into the hallway as Rio and Zane follow us. "We need to head out. We have a long road trip ahead of us."

"Road trip?"

Zane speaks up. "You thought that car was a rental?"

"Well . . . yeah," I reply.

Zane smirks. "You know what they say when you assume."

"Time to hit the road!" Rio shouts and hops in the car, followed by Asher, who rolls his eyes at Rio's overenthusiasm.

The blood drains from my face. I love these men like crazy, but twenty-four hours in a car with all three of them . . . I don't know how I'm going to survive. I'm sure they'll find something for us to do to pass the time.

CHAPTER 33

SPENCER

Dropping the cardboard box, I sink into the couch. It's still comfortable even if it's covered in plastic wrap. Thankfully, there wasn't much of a debate when I told Asher that I wasn't going to give up my couch. Everyone agreed that my sectional was more comfortable.

"That box is labeled 'bedroom.'" Zane plops down next to me.

I raise my brow, handing out sass like it's Halloween candy. "And?"

Zane places an arm behind me, along the back of the couch. "And this is our new living room. Not your bedroom."

"Well, if you're so concerned about it, then you can move it to the bedroom."

Zane holds back a smile. "It's possible I could be convinced to carry out that act of service."

"Who's being serviced?" Rio pokes his head into the room.

"Oh my God!" I laugh so hard that I swear I'm going to pee my pants.

Asher walks in carrying three boxes stacked on top of each other and sets them down. "What's going on in here?"

"Apparently, there was going to be some *servicing*," Rio speculates.

"I think we've all done our fair share of that last night and this morning. In fact, because of all the servicing going on around here, it's taken us three days to move into our new house." Asher places his hands on his hips as he scolds us.

I was ready to scream at all of them after a few days in my apartment, but I held it together. We were practically living on top of each other. I was able to handle it before, when I thought the living situation was temporary. I figured once everything was over, they'd go back to their brownstone. But instead, Rio declared that they were moving in. My response was to scream and threaten to throw all their things out the window and onto the street.

Yeah, that was me holding it together.

Thankfully, Asher had a solution: buy a new place big enough for all of us. We found the perfect place in the Bronx, close to Paloma. She always fills our fridge with an all-you-can-eat buffet. Unfortunately, it took us months to find our new home. But we're here now and I love it.

Standing, I wave my hands defensively. "Hey, now, I'm not the one at fault here."

Zane scoffs. "No need to lie. You're the one who always incites it."

"What! Not true!"

"You're in denial, Mama. It's not a pretty place to be."

"Ha ha. Very funny," I snap.

Zane stands and Rio joins him. Asher saunters over as well. They all cross their arms as they stare at me like I'm their every fantasy come to life.

"The first one to catch me gets to come first." I wink and sprint for the staircase.

Laughter follows me, and I hear Rio exclaim, "We need to put a ring on it ASAP."

EPILOGUE

DAHLIA

Reaching high above my head, I set the last mug in the cupboard. I look around at my new apartment while August plays with his toy trucks that Hayes bought him. In fact, Hayes purchased most of what we needed to furnish the apartment, much to my chagrin.

Unpacking is a bitch—not that we had much to begin with.

There's a knock on the door, and I immediately pull out the gun I have hidden on the top shelf of the cupboard.

"Baby, take those to your room and play."

"Okay, Mommy." August struggles to gather the trucks in his chubby little arms.

I can't believe he just turned three.

There's another knock after August shuts the door to his room. I approach on quiet feet and squint, looking through the peephole.

"Open up, Dahlia. I know you're in there."

Oh my hell.

Keeping the chain lock in place, I open the door a couple of inches. "What do you want, Hayes?"

"Can we talk, please?"

Resisting his crystal blue eyes is impossible. They're my kryptonite.

"I'm not going to change my mind."

His dejected puppy look is a kick straight to the gut. "I know."

I yield to his request and undo the chain lock, letting him inside, but I don't move further into the apartment. I don't want him to think this is a long visit.

He gives the gun in my hand a questioning look.

"I'm a single mom living in the city," I explain. It's not a lie, but not the whole truth.

He raises his brows, letting me know he sees right through my bullshit. But he doesn't push the question further. He scans the room and asks, "Where's August?"

"Playing with his trucks in his room. Thank you again for getting those for him."

"Of course." He gives me a small smile then turns more serious. "In Boston, you said we couldn't be together because it wasn't safe."

"That's right."

"But Anthony Cole is dead. Pierce Murphy is long gone. Isn't it safe now?"

Pinching my lips together, I think through my answer. "No, it's not. I'm sorry."

I wish I could say yes. I wish I was a normal young adult. I wish I didn't have the thought of my upbringing looming over my head.

But one day, The Company will come for me. They'll find out where I am and expect me to pay my dues, and I can't let Hayes get on The Company's radar. They'll use and exploit him to get me to do what they want. I already had one psycho do that to my son. I can't let that happen again.

Mother always said that to love is to show weakness. She made sure I learned my lesson over and over. If only she could see me now, with a son and a man I'm completely in love with.

"Why not?"

Sealing my heart behind a metal door, I prepare myself for this conversation. "There are other people who want to find me. Because of them, it's not safe."

"Who?" he insists.

"I can't tell you."

His jaw tightens in frustration. "Can't, or won't?"

"Can't."

Hayes runs his hands through his hair and paces back and forth for a moment. "You're not the only one with secrets, you know."

"I know."

He's getting flustered. He came here to convince me that we should stay together, but my mind is made up. If I never want The Company to find out about Hayes, then I need to create some distance.

My hands clasp behind my back to prevent myself from reaching for him, even though I'm desperate to fall in his arms. "I knew from the beginning that you were hiding something, but I decided that I didn't need to know because I couldn't share my own."

"While we were in Boston, did you . . ."

"Yeah. I heard Kieran call you 'Declan' one night when I was looking for you." I shrug.

Hayes—*Declan* rubs the back of his neck and sighs. "My father is—"

"I know. Once I heard your last name, I knew," I interrupt him.

"How?"

Biting my lip, my eyes dart away from his. "Don't ask me that, please."

Declan's lips twist into a frown. "Why weren't you afraid?"

"I knew you'd keep us safe," I answer sincerely.

He reaches for me. His hands cup my cheeks, and he rests his head against mine. "Just don't shut me out. I can't handle that." His honesty punches me in the gut.

"I won't," I whisper.

"You still going to show up for work at Abstract Dreams?"

Letting out a sarcastic laugh, I reply, "Definitely. It's my only legitimate work experience, and I don't have a sugar daddy to live off of."

His smile is sad. Then he wraps his arms around my shoulders and pulls me close. I bury my face in his chest and finally allow a single tear to slip free.

When he lets go, he darts for the door, as if he'll cave if he stays a moment longer.

"Bye, Dahlia. See you tomorrow."

My real name on his lips is a shot to the heart. He knows some of my darkest moments, and he still wants to be with me.

"Goodbye, Declan."

EPILOGUE 2

SPENCER, TWO YEARS LATER

"*I*f I had known this would feel like a million kittens scratching me all at once, I wouldn't have wanted to get one."

Buzzzzz. Buzzzzz. Buzzzzz.

"You're doing fine, Mama. Just relax."

Buzzzzz. Buzzzzz. Buzzzzz.

Lifting my head, I glare at Asher and give his hand an extra squeeze. "Why didn't you tell me it'd be this irritating?"

Asher doesn't even flinch at the pain I'm trying to inflict. Instead, he rolls his eyes at my constant whining. "I did tell you. We talked about it a lot . . . *in detail.*"

"I'm almost done. Don't worry." Rio attempts to placate me but ultimately fails.

Buzzzzz. Buzzzzz. Buzzzzz.

Soon after our cross-country road trip from Texas, I told the guys that I wanted a tattoo. They were all supportive but very adamant that they'd kill whoever laid hands on me, even if it was for something as simple as a tattoo. They only amended their threat to say that Joey didn't count. I may have made some threats myself, which led to Rio deciding to learn how to tattoo.

Rio spent most of his free time over the last year and a half as an apprentice for a local tattoo artist. A week ago, he finally came to me and said he was ready to give me my first tattoo. I gave him complete creative control. My only stipulation was that the tattoo be something that would remind me of all of them, which is how I found myself lying on my stomach, topless, while Rio tattoos my spine.

I tried to argue that I would be cold and uncomfortable. Rio's solution was that he and Asher take off their shirts to make it fair. He completely misunderstood me. So now I'm cold, uncomfortable, and horny.

Not a fun combination.

"Okay, Mama. All done." Rio shuts off his machine and sits back.

"Finally," I complain. Sitting up, I forget that my boobs are completely free. Asher gives me his "come hither" look, and my stomach flutters. I'll never get used to that look.

Scrambling to get off the table, I flash Rio as well, and he gives me a whistle of appreciation. "No need to thank me so generously," he teases.

"Oh, shut up," I retort. Covering my breasts with my arm, I scurry over to the mirror in our entryway. Tears well up in my eyes as I examine the masterpiece Rio has etched on my skin. "It's beautiful, but I don't understand how this is supposed to be about you."

Rio's reflection joins mine in the mirror. "It's not about us. It's about you."

My lips twist into a perplexed frown. "I don't understand."

"You don't need to be reminded of us. We're already right

here." Leaning down, Rio kisses my hand where it rests over my heart. "Sometimes we forget who we are and what we are capable of, so I wanted you to have a permanent reminder of that.

Rio steps to the side and very lightly trails his fingers over the design. "Roses for love, beauty, and passion—to remind you that you are the most beautiful woman we've ever loved. Lavender for calm—to remind you not to give in to fear. Daisies for new beginnings—to remind you that you can always start over and keep going. Irises for courage—to remind you that you are brave."

Asher joins us and wipes away the tears trickling down my face.

"What about the script?" My lip wobbles.

His finger traces each letter, sending a shiver down my spine. "*Yo soy fuerte*. I am strong. *Yo soy hermosa*. I am beautiful. *Yo soy una diabla*. I am a devil."

Blinking away more tears, I sniffle in the most unattractive way. "Damn you, Navarro Flores." A small chuckle escapes me. "It's absolutely perfect. Thank you."

The front door bangs open and I squeal, diving into the living room to hide my half naked body from whoever just barged in.

"Angel!"

"Zane?" I poke my head around the corner. "What are you doing? You gave me a heart attack."

Zane is panting like he just ran here all the way from the precinct. "She called."

"Sharon?"

"Yes! She called. She said she has twin girls who need long-term placement and that they'll be here in an hour."

Oh my God. It's happening.

After seeing Zane with Margaret and how Rio and Asher were gentle with Noah and August, we talked about becoming foster parents. The process to be approved was long and difficult.

Seriously. How was I supposed to explain to the social worker that I'm in a relationship with all three of them and two of them are together too?

Surprisingly, it went over well. With Zane being NYPD, Asher being FBI, and Rio being a former prosecutor, the social worker said we are more than capable of keeping children safe. Zane was more than excited to become a foster dad. Asher was timid, but it has grown on him. And Rio is always down for any and every adventure.

Sharon did multiple walk-throughs of our home, which Zane and Asher were very intense about baby proofing. We even did some renovations. We knocked down a wall between two of the bedrooms to make one large room for all four of us to share and the other two rooms are for whatever children the state of New York needs us to care for. I thought sharing a room would be stifling, but I've actually enjoyed it. But what sealed the deal for me was when Rio brought the huge mattress from my old apartment. I love the huge cuddle sessions.

And now we finally get to put those extra rooms to use.

My eyes go wide as I realize I'm still holding my boobs. "Shit! We need to get dressed!"

We all scramble to clean up, put shirts on, and get the rooms ready as Zane tells us about the conversation he had with Sharon. She said the four-year-old twins were found in a crack house hiding in a bedroom closet while their mother was high out of her mind.

An hour later, on the dot, the doorbell rings, and nerves take over my body.

Asher grabs my hands and blocks my view of the front door. "Hey, it's okay. We're ready for this."

"What if I'm a bad mom? What if I hurt them, and I don't mean to?" I stare at his chest, but I'm not actually seeing what's in front of me. Instead, I'm envisioning every possible scenario in which I fuck up.

Asher tilts my chin so I'm looking up into his eyes. "I think every parent worries about that—it means you care. The best thing we can do for these girls is make sure they feel loved and safe. We can do this."

"Okay," I whisper.

Zane opens the door eagerly with Rio right behind him. "Hi, Sharon!" He crouches down so he's level with two little girls. One has two long braids, and the other has two high pigtails. They hold each other's hand firmly as if they're afraid they'll be separated. "And this must be Ana and Sofia."

"I'm Sofia," the one with pigtails answers. "Mrs. Sharon said you're FBI. Is that true? What does FBI mean?"

"Oh, I'm not FBI—he is." Zane points to Asher. "I'm a New York detective."

Sofia frowns and tilts her head to the side. "What's a dee-tet-uh-tive?"

Zane makes a welcoming gesture. "Do you want to come inside, and I'll tell you all about it?"

Sofia squints her sweet brown eyes at Zane, then examines the rest of us. "Does Ana get to come too?"

"Yes, of course."

Sofia lets out a sigh of relief and nods. "Okay, we'll stay then."

"I'll let you all get settled in. Call me if you have any questions." Sharon sets the girls' bags inside the door and waves goodbye.

"Do you want to see your room?" Rio asks Sofia.

"Can Ana stay in there with me?"

Rio scoffs dramatically in jest. "Well, duh. The room has bunk beds."

For the first time, Ana shows emotion with a large smile and nods enthusiastically. We lead them upstairs and get them situated.

While showing them the room, I sit on the floor and pull out the dolls, blocks, and other toys they get to play with. Ana walks straight to me and plops down on my lap. My chest fills with warmth as this innocent soul gives her trust to me. She puts a doll in my hand and grabs one for herself, then talks for her doll, pretending they're about to go play at a park.

I look up to find Asher, Rio, and Zane staring at me with various expressions of excitement and adoration.

Asher sits down next to us and grabs a doll for himself while Sofia pulls Rio and Zane onto the floor to play with the blocks.

This is the life I chose for myself. This is the life I get to keep choosing every day.

Want to see where Raven ends up? Preorder your copy of *Dark Whispers* HERE or scan the QR code below!

Wondering about the serial killer named John the Baptist?
Guess what? He had a daughter. Savannah's story is revealed in
Silence in the Snow! Preorder your copy HERE or scan the QR
code below!

ACKNOWLEDGMENTS

My other half— Thank you for always being willing to reach things on the top shelf. Thank you for letting me attach myself like a koala to a tree when I need comfort. Thank you for reminding me of my power and strength. You are my touchstone and my safe harbor. I love you.

My favourite Canadian—Thank you for teaching me how to properly spell "favourite." I'm sorry that being my PA has fucked with the autocorrect on your phone. And thank you for always reminding me that I deserve the same grace that I show to others. Thank you for letting me show you my crazy book collection and thank you for showing me yours. Our crazies match perfectly. Love you!

Savannah—Thank you for being willing to combine our crazy hordes of crotch goblins for dinner on the nights my sanity is ready to take a permanent leave of absence. Thank you for the quiet, comforting space you always hold for me. Thank you for listening without judgment. Thank you for being that friend that pushes me outside my comfort zone. Thank you for making me feel safe enough to cry. I love you something fierce.

Alexys—Thank you for your unconditional support. Thank you for teaching me that I don't need to constantly apologize for everything little thing. Thank you for always making sure I feel loved and valued. Thank you for your pep talks and addicting me to plants. Love you!

My ride-or-die—Thank you for sticking with me, through thick and thin. Over two thousand miles apart yet we're solid as fuck. Eighteen years in the books and here's to eighteen more. Love you!

Ashli and Beth—We're a crazy trio, but a fun trio. Our book talks, mom talks, and tea sessions are my favourite. Thank you for encouraging me and hyping me up every step of the way. And thank you for the crazy spreadsheets. FYI, they're not that crazy. Love y'all!

Kelli—Thank you for your unending support and being a friend I can talk to about anything. You validate me in all my feelings and wild whims. Love you!

My siblings—Mom and Dad still don't know. Keep it that way.

Bookstagrammers, Booktokkers, and Influencers—Thank you for reading, reviewing, sharing, etc. The Devils of New York series would not be here without your support. Stay smutty!

The Assholes Who Took From Me—This series is partly for you. For all the times you made me feel afraid. For all the times you made me believe that no one else would want me. For all the times you made me think that no one would believe my truth. For all the times I was crying on the bathroom floor because I thought I was worthless or that I deserved it. For all the times my husband had to comfort me because I had a flash-back. Disrespectfully, fuck you.

STAY CONNECTED

You can find Ivy in all the bookish places…
Website
Newsletter
Ivy's Spicy Harem (Facebook Reader Group)
Instagram
Goodreads
BookBub
Amazon
Pinterest
Threads

ABOUT THE AUTHOR

Ivy King is a why choose dark romance author who lives in the mountains of Idaho with her book husband, four wild kids, and cuddly pitbull. When Ivy isn't writing smut, you can find her tending to her emotional support houseplants, wrapped in a fluffy blanket reading romance novels, doom scrolling on her phone, or watching true crime.